Match!

COLLEEN MacGILCHRIST
with
BOB MacGILCHRIST

SIMPLE STRATEGIES *for* HAPPILY EVER AFTER

A Relationship Parable

ABINTRA PUBLISHING

Match!: Simple Strategies for Happily Ever After

Colleen MacGilchrist with Bob MacGilchrist
First Edition 2003

Copyright © 2003 by Colleen MacGilchrist

ISBN: 0-9722359-0-6
Library of Congress Control Number: 2002096237

Cover design: Paddy Bruce
Text design and typography: Paddy Bruce

Published by Abintra Publishing
P. O. Box 456
Bellingham, WA 98227

All rights reserved. This book may not be reproduced in whole or in part, or transmitted in any form, without written permission from the publisher, except by a reviewer who may quote brief passages in a review; nor may any part of this book be reproduced, stored in a retrieval system, or transmitted in any form or by any means electronic, mechanical, photocopying, recording, or other, without written permission from the publisher.

Publisher's Note:
This publication is designed to provide information in regard to relationships with the understanding that the publisher is not engaged in rendering psychological services. If expert assistance or counseling is needed, the services of a competent professional should be sought.

Note on Quotations:
The quotations have been gleaned from a variety of sources over the years: speakers, books, posters and the Internet and attributed by the same. Every effort was made to confirm the accuracy of the quotes and the veracity of the attributions, however, they may not be accurate as many are obscure and not found in reference standards.

For all of the couples who have shared their triumphs and challenges with us and for the many mentors who have guided us through their examples and words, both written and spoken. We have been blessed by you all.

Acknowledgments

We wish to thank Dawn Groves who took us under her wing and walked with us through the arduous process of rewriting. Her work as editor, dear friend and encourager proved invaluable. Without Dawn there would be no book. We also want to thank Dawn's husband, Dan Barrett and daughters, Holly and Samantha, who loaned us their wife and mother for an innumerable number of hours, days and months.

Thanks also to Amanda DuBois and Carla Marsh who were present at the conception and offered support all along the way including reading and critiquing. As final readers Dan Barrett, Gary Blessington, Katie Elliott, Edie Harris, JP MacConnell, Mark MacGilchrist, Brenda Rogers and Sandy Shipley worked diligently and incisively to complete the process. All of the above generously gave of their time and talent without recompense.

And a final thanks to our incredible artist, Paddy Bruce. Paddy read the manuscript, attended the workshop and embraced the project with enthusiasm. Her artistry and heart wrapped this book in beauty and love.

Match!

Contents

PART I
Happily Ever After	2
Seeking Solutions	6
Is This For Me	7
The Power of Commitment	14
Trust Me	19
The Blame Game	24
Just Listen	27

PART II
Retreating	36
Clear Intention	43
Relationship Evolution	46
Vows	51
Love Letters	54
Turbulence	55
Preference and Style Differences	61
Gracious Listening	68
Connections or Collisions	71
Do Overs	81
Inner Dialogue	84
Walking the Heart Path	92
Inside-Out Communication	98
Heart Path Solutions	104
Commitment	109
Passion and Spirituality	115
Questions and Answers	119
Nurture	123
EPILOGUE	130
AFTERWORD	132

Figures

Figure 1	Divorce Statistics	45
Figure 2	Relationship Evolution	48
Figure 3	SAFE Number	49
Figure 4	Preferences and Style Differences	63
Figure 5	Art of Gracious Listening	70
Figure 6	Feeling Words	87
Figure 7	Walking the Heart Path	91
Figure 8	Intentional Gifts for Sarah	127

Match!

PART I

Happily Ever After

Marriage and war, thought Sarah as she struggled out of her dripping raincoat. No difference in my family. "Heeere kitty!" she called, slinging her purse over a kitchen chair. The condo seemed emptier than usual except for the silent blink of the answering machine.

"Oh joy, messages," she muttered, pressing the playback button. "Happy birthday to yoouuuuuu," the answering machine squawked.

Sarah smiled and glanced at a faded photo pinned to her corkboard. It was a wallet-sized image of two little girls blowing out ten birthday candles. Twenty years later and good old Lynda still couldn't carry a tune. She shook her head at the memory, massaging her left shoulder.

She pressed the stop button. The other messages could wait. Grabbing a pint of mocha chip gelato from the freezer, she rummaged around for one of her grandmother's sterling silver spoons. A gray

Match!

blur darted past her as she headed for the couch, spoon already in her mouth. A tiny Persian cat glared from the side table next to the phone.

"Geez, I didn't mean to startle you, Sophie."

Sarah dropped into the cushions and Sophie tiptoed across the armrest. Sarah pulled the spoon from her mouth and squinted toward the kitchen clock. Midnight. "I wish I could talk to Lynda," she said, absently twisting a strand of blond hair between her thumb and forefinger. "Hey, it's my 30th birthday. I'm allowed." Juggling the ice cream carton and Sophie, she grabbed the phone from the side table and punched in a phone number. It rang four times before a voice whispered, "Hullo...?"

Sarah heard covers rustling.

"Hey Lynda, you awake?" she asked.

"Oh Sarah. What's so important at...good Lord, it's *late!*"

"I'm sorry but I really need to talk."

A few more rustles and then, "Okay, I'm not awake but I can fake it."

"Will we disturb Dave?"

"Dave can sleep through anything," said Lynda. "Talk to me."

"It's Mike; he proposed again."

"This is bad?" Lynda yawned.

"He took me to a special restaurant—romantic, delicious. Just after the shrimp bisque he held my hand, popped open a little black box from La Mirage and whispered, 'Marry me.' I froze. I couldn't breathe."

Match!

"Ouch! What did he do?"

"He was quiet the rest of the evening. There was a look in his eyes. I think he might be ready to give up. We're obviously mismatched. He's a great guy and I'm a coward. He deserves someone who'd jump at the chance to marry him." Sarah shoved in another spoonful of ice cream.

"Time out. What are you eating?"

Sarah shivered as she swallowed. "Why do you ask?"

"When was the last time you called me late at night without a carton of ice cream in your hand?"

"So? It soothes me." Sarah unbuttoned her waistband. "See what a mess I am?" She propped her long legs on the coffee table.

"You're not a mess," Lynda's voice was quiet, "but you are medicating. Eating won't solve your problems."

"Early survival training," mumbled Sarah staring into the carton. "The thought of getting married gives me the willies. My parents hate each other; my brother and sister are both divorced. My odds are terrible."

"I know, I know," sighed Lynda. " But you're not like everyone else in your family. You and Mike are a great match. Hey, he's met your parents so he knows why you're chicken."

"Honest to God, sometimes when Mike and I disagree I feel like screaming at him. Then I'd sound like my mother."

"You're not your mother. She's a drama queen."

"And you think I can be different?"

"You are different," said Lynda. "When you make your

Match!

mind up, you can do anything. I've seen it."

"Okay." Sarah set the carton down on the carpet. Sophie scrambled after it, shoving her head inside. "I guess I feel better. You should get back to sleep now."

"Ah, the voice of reason returns."

"Thanks." Sarah shifted to hang up the phone but stopped mid-reach. "Wait a minute!"

"Did I really believe you were finished?"

"I almost forgot, Mike wants me to go with him to some couple's retreat. It's called a relationship renewal. It's the weekend after Valentine's Day. Relationship renewal. Valentine's Day...isn't that too cute?"

"I wanna go," Lynda whined.

"Mike probably hopes I'll hang around happy couples and catch the fever."

"Sounds like Mike's onto something—learn how to be in a relationship before you move in together. What a novel idea."

"Like I can learn? What on earth does a guy like that see in me?" Sarah tucked the phone between her chin and shoulder, grabbed Sophie and started power combing clumps of winter fur.

"What's not to love? You're smart, beautiful, you have a great career and excellent taste in friends." Lynda yawned again. "I'm going back to sleep now. I love you, Mike loves you. Happy birthday and goodnight."

People need to see themselves as miracles and worthy of love.
VIRGINIA SATIR

Match!

Sarah hung up the phone. Maybe Lynda was right. Maybe she could overcome the family curse. Grabbing her current mystery novel, she headed for the bedroom.

"C'mon Sophie, time to call it a night."

Seeking Solutions

Sarah sat at her kitchen table folding the laundry. Ah, the Sunday afternoon countdown. Sarah was gearing up at work for the annual meeting in April, busy overseeing the year-end reports from accounting. She straightened a stack of towels and studied her corkboard covered with photos: Mike and his dog Rex, Mike on the soccer field, Mike and Sarah at the beach. His Italian good looks—olive skin, chiseled arms and curly brown hair contrasted nicely with her tidy Nordic features. She smiled at the hint of a receding hairline—his only point of vanity. She imagined him in front of his middle schoolers. Anyone who could face that sea of raging hormones every day had to be made of good stuff.

Mike emerged from the bedroom zipping his duffel bag. "Gotta go," he said.

"Already?" Sarah loved their weekends together as long as it didn't include a marriage certificate and offspring.

"I have papers to correct and lesson plans to write." He rooted through the hall closet with casual self-consciousness, avoiding her gaze. He'd been distant all weekend.

"We still haven't talked about what happened at dinner

Match!

the other night."

"Yeah, I guess we've both been avoiding it." He dropped onto the chair beside her.

"Are you mad at me?" Sarah studied her fingernails.

"I'm frustrated. It feels like we're at an impasse." Mike rested his elbows on the table and massaged his temples.

"Where do we go from here?" Sarah folded her hands on the table, her shoulders tense.

He looked up at her. "We've been through this before, Sarah. I don't want to lose you but sitting on the fence isn't working. The couples retreat might help." He took her hand and looked into her eyes. "Please talk to Kate—you'll like her and she knows her stuff." Mike had mentioned Kate Wallace before. She was the co-facilitator of the retreat.

Sarah held Mike's gaze. "Okay, I'll call her." She leaned over and gave him a slow, warm kiss. He reluctantly stood up, smiling. "You're the love of my life, you know." He tapped her nose lightly.

"Ditto," she said, the tension broken.

Mike pulled a business card from his wallet, handing it to Sarah. "Just call Kate, okay?"

"Tomorrow, I promise," said Sarah, waving the card as he disappeared down the hallway. She missed him already.

Is This for Me

Sarah pushed back from her office desk. She stared out the window at the glass and steel building across the street,

turning Kate's business card over between her fingers. Mike seemed so set on this relationship retreat. Was he expecting her to bare her soul in front of a bunch of strangers? And this Kate—probably some relationship Nazi. Sarah forced herself to dial the number.

"Hello," said a soft voice.

"Oh hello, I'm Sarah Grady calling for Kate Wallace."

"This is Kate."

"Hi, I'm dating Mike Mascori. I think he told you I'd be calling for an appointment."

"Yes, Sarah." Kate sounded pleased. "I'm looking forward to getting together. Let's see…I have 6 p.m. open this Thursday. Would that work for you?"

Sarah checked her calendar. She swallowed hard. "Okay." At least it was four days away.

Thursday evening Sarah joined the throng of cars crawling outbound across the West Seattle Bridge. She turned onto a narrow, winding street. Homes ancient to new dotted the wooded hillside. Through the trees she glimpsed lights sparkling on Elliott Bay. Sarah parked in front of a shingled, 1980's, Northwest contemporary. Grabbing her coat and purse, she hurried down a slate footpath bordered by cedars, vine maples, ferns and bamboo. A wind chime tinkled in the breeze. Maybe this won't be so bad, she thought, knocking on the sage green door.

A petite woman wearing navy cords and a woolly sweater opened the door. She looked to be in her mid-

fifties with short salt and pepper hair and minimal make-up. "You must be Sarah," she said, her eyes smiled as she extended a work-worn, gardener's hand. "Glad you made it through the traffic, I'm Kate."

Thank goodness, no hug. Kate led her into a private sitting room with hardwood floors and an oriental rug. A bookcase filled one wall. Relationship books lined several shelves. That many books for couples—who knew?

Kate motioned toward an overstuffed chair. Sarah perched at the edge of the cushion as Kate settled on the loveseat across from her.

"It's so nice to finally meet you, Sarah." Kate rested her feet on the round coffee table. "Mike talks about you. All good."

"Mike mentioned he'd been working on a school project with you," said Sarah. "He's so involved with the kids I lose track."

"It's called the Awareness Project," Kate explained. "We're attempting to teach middle schoolers about relationships. But you're here to find out about the retreat. Mike wants to go and you're not so sure."

"That's right. I have a few questions."

"Mike told me you're pretty thorough so fire away."

"Well, I know a little bit about your background. Mike said that you're a pastoral counselor and that your husband, Jim, is a marriage and family therapist."

"Our focus is helping people experience fulfilling, long-lasting relationships. We believe that healing conflict on the planet begins with better conflict resolution at home."

 Match!

"Is conflict an inevitable part of a relationship?"

"Until humankind takes a huge evolutionary leap, I'm afraid so. The good news is that intimacy actually deepens when we become willing to talk about our problems and listen with an open heart."

"Then you think conflict is good?" Sarah asked, surprised.

"It can be. It's how you handle it that makes the difference. Most of us are too afraid or reactive. That's where the retreat comes in. We give you tools to work with conflict and actually evolve through it."

"Mike thinks the retreat would be good for us but I don't know." Sarah's voice trailed off. "I'm...I'm a private person. I don't want to share my innermost feelings with a group of strangers." Sarah noticed the familiar tightness in her left shoulder.

Kate smiled. "You can set that concern aside. During the course of the retreat, the only sharing you need to do is with your partner. Jim and I will talk about relationships in a series of presentations to the group and then we'll assign a few exercises. The exercises are private."

"So I won't have to talk in front of anyone?" Sarah gave herself a little shoulder massage.

"Not unless you want to. Perhaps you would

We look forward to the time when the power to love will replace the love of power. Then will our world know the blessings of peace.
WILLIAM E. GLADSTONE

feel better if you talked to couples that have already been through the retreat. Before you leave I'll give you a list of references. You can call them and ask questions."

"I'd like that, thanks." Sarah slipped off her shoes and put her feet up on the table. "Can you tell me a little bit more about the content of the retreat?"

"Well," said Kate, "over many years Jim and I have noticed key values and practices that strengthen and deepen relationships. We've distilled them into a few simple practices that focus on nurturing, commitment and communication."

"But Mike and I already do that. I'm committed. I just don't want to get married. Why would we need a weekend retreat to teach us what we already know?" Sarah asked.

"It's not about teaching; it's about practicing. Even though we do these things in the beginning, old habits and reactions emerge as relationships mature. We stop talking because we're afraid of what we'll say, we stop listening because we're afraid of what we'll hear, we become too distracted to show our love on a regular basis and in the end, our commitment is eroded."

"I admit that there are times when I'm not entirely honest with Mike. I feel like I have to keep a lid on my dark side, so to speak. I didn't grow up in a family that talked about the big stuff." Sarah smiled grimly.

"Most of us didn't. We all have to learn how to be in a relationship. Some more than others."

Sarah leaned forward. "My parents argue over everything. My sister and brother are already divorced. I

Match!

feel like I'm doomed to failure."

"You're not doomed, Sarah." Kate's voice was warm. "Yes, you learned destructive relationship habits at home. However, as an adult you can choose to do something different."

"How?" Sarah almost pleaded. "Just choose again? That's new age jargon. It's not that easy."

"Of course it's not easy. But the tools we'll give you at the retreat will help you nurture your relationship over the long haul. And when you revert to old habits—which we all do on occasion—you won't judge yourself so harshly."

"I'll change my family pattern after one weekend?"

"You'll have a start."

Sarah sighed and shook her head. "Why is it that people meet, fall in love and then usually end up unhappy or separated? Is it possible to have a long and happy relationship?"

"Jim and I are happy and we've been together for many years."

"So it's been easy for you?"

"Oh no." Kate laughed, "We've both been divorced and had more than a few lousy relationships."

"How is this one different?"

"We decided that our marriage was not only going to survive, it was going to flourish. We learned how to move through conflict, even use the conflict to grow."

"Why can't two people who say they love each other just get along?"

Kate grinned. "That's the age-old question. I don't have

the answer to it, but I do have an opinion. We can't get along for two reasons: First we're reacting to our negative emotions and personal history instead of responding to what's happening now. Second, when the inevitable conflicts do arise, we don't know how to resolve them in an effective way.

"In the beginning of a romance, differences in personality and preferences are seen as charming. But when the heat of new love cools, the differences cause conflict. The romantic phase of a relationship is like a free sample that comes in the mail with a coupon for more. You cash in the coupon by forming a strong bond with each other based on commitment and mutual respect. Then through inspiration, education and practice you become skillful at resolving conflict together."

"So conflict is unavoidable but it doesn't have to tear us apart," said Sarah.

"If you take responsibility for thinking and acting in ways that support a great relationship you'll evolve through the conflict and deepen your connection to each other. You see, your partnership is actually a spiritual path for personal transformation; a path two people walk side-by-side. Conflict, differences in temperament and style, your personal goals and even shared dreams all create opportunities to become more peaceful and loving, inside and out."

At the end of their visit Kate handed Sarah the list of references. Sarah wondered if calling them was a stalling tactic. No, she needed to do the research.

Match!

The Power of Commitment

Saturday morning found Sarah at a neighborhood bakery in the University district. She was meeting a couple from Kate's reference list: Emily and George. It was a sunny Seattle day; the trees were bare, the air chilly. As she pushed through the door her lungs filled with the aroma of fresh-baked bread. Wood booths and an uneven planked floor echoed the 1970's. Across the room Sarah spied a couple matching Emily's phone description—plump and plumper in their sixties. "Emily?"

"Sarah? Come sit down." Emily's round face widened with a smile. Her sparse brown hair seemed lush compared to George's shiny bald head. "Have breakfast with us, dear."

Sarah ordered the ginger waffle and coffee with cream. Emily's eyebrows shot up. "You must come from a family with skinny genes!"

"And a love of all things sweet," Sarah admitted, handing the menu to the waitress.

George and Emily ordered oatmeal with non-fat milk and orange juice. They were a chatty couple; finishing each other's sentences in between bites.

Eventually Sarah got around to talking about the retreat. "So what benefits did you get from the weekend?" she asked.

George smiled and drew Emily close, "The biggest benefit is that, ten years later we're still together. We were in our 50's on the brink of divorce when we went to the

Match!

first retreat. Emily's attorney suggested we do it. Can you believe that?" George laughed.

Emily jumped in. "I figured George would go. He goes along with most things."

"The divorce was Emily's idea," said George, "but I suppose I was convincing her she was right. I was so used to Emily being out with the kids that I just parked in front of the tube and channel surfed. Emily tried to find something we could do together but I'd gone on autopilot."

"That made me..." Emily started.

"...crazy!" George cut in. "Emily wanted out. I didn't care except for the hassle and the dough."

Emily poked her finger into George's round belly. "Yep, I married a zombie. But then I'd been so busy with my own job and the kids that it was good not to have him underfoot. Now I was facing retirement with the living dead. I was ready for adventure and he was ready for bed."

"Wow, sounds like a recipe for disaster," said Sarah. "What changed things?"

"Well, the retreat, for starters," said Emily.

"Yeah, there was no TV," laughed George. "We had to talk to each other. That was new. And I was really hit hard by the part about fully committing to the relationship."

Emily continued, "That commitment piece was important. I'd spent the last ten years convinced that I'd married the wrong guy. My

The most precious gift we can offer others is our presence. When mindfulness embraces those we love, they will bloom like flowers.
THICH NHAT HANH

Match!

periscope was up, searching for my..." Emily made quotation marks with her fingers, "...soul mate." She chuckled at herself. "It drained energy from the relationship leaving George pretty much in the cold."

"Don't be hard on yourself, sweetheart. I didn't warm things up." George patted her leg.

Emily put her hand over George's and gave it an affectionate squeeze. "When they asked us to commit to our partners physically, mentally and emotionally—just through the weekend—we agreed to try it. We hadn't been present for each other in years. It was a turning point," said Emily.

Sarah squirmed as they talked. The words 'turning point' helped her settle back into her chair.

"We actually enjoyed each other that weekend. We talked," said George.

"...and listened," said Emily. "We discovered that we both wanted to travel in Europe."

"I was an expert from watching travel shows on PBS," George winked. "See, all that TV wasn't so bad!"

Emily slid closer to George. "I'll admit you're a helluva travel guide and a soft pillow during those long train rides."

Emily and George went on to explain how they were especially pleased that their married children had adopted some of their new communication skills. They considered it their best legacy. It was good to meet a couple who still loved each other after being married for over 40 years. Sarah thanked them for their time and the breakfast. Emily insisted on paying.

 Match!

As Sarah drove home she turned up the radio, singing along with the oldies. Maybe marriage wasn't so bad. Pulling into her parking space, she spotted Mike's burgundy Jeep at the curb. She bounded up the stairs clutching a box from the bakery. "Mike!" she called, throwing the front door open. Sophie skittered across the kitchen floor. "Where is he, Soph?" Sarah checked the empty hook next to the hall closet. "Ah, the leash is missing. Giving you a break from the big dog?"

Moments later a young golden retriever hurtled through the front door, tail at full throttle. Mike followed, windblown. "We're all glad you're home," he smiled, hanging up the leash and planting a kiss on her cheek.

"Look what I brought you," Sarah sang, opening the bakery box and showing off a glistening cinnamon roll.

"Looks decadent," he said. "Only one?"

"Yeah, I was full when I left the bakery."

"I'll share." Mike took the box.

"No, no," she waved him off, "I had a ginger waffle. Want a latte?"

Mike brewed fresh espresso and then Sarah steamed the milk. Mugs in hand, they relaxed on the rug in front of the fireplace. Sarah's eyes danced as she talked about her visit with George and Emily.

"They were so great. They'd almost divorced and then went to the retreat and swear it was a turning point. They recommitted to each other. They seem really happy."

"Mmm..." mumbled Mike through a mouthful of cinnamon roll. He noticed Sarah eyeing the pastry as he

Match!

brought it up to his mouth.

"Can I have some?" she asked.

He stopped mid-bite, "Good thing there's another bakery down the street."

Sarah licked her lips and sipped the latte, suddenly quiet.

"Hey there," Mike said, running his finger down the crease between her eyebrows. "Where'd you go?"

Where there is great love, there are always miracles.
WILLA CATHER

"I was thinking about my family," she said. "Dad would come home from work, turn on the news, eat dinner in silence unless he was on Mom's hot-seat. He was physically present but mentally and emotionally, somewhere else."

She drew her legs under her. "Then my brother got married and one kid later they split. He spent his time on the golf course while his wife got her exercise walking from the car to the mall. At least Dad was physically present; Jeff wasn't present at all."

Mike rubbed her shoulder. "And your point is?"

"It worries me that I'll fall into my family pattern if we get married. I might turn into a shrew or check out completely. Kate told me I could decide to be different but there's more to change than just making a decision. Those patterns are buried pretty deep. I don't know how to change them."

Match!

"You can, Sarah. Your family may be relationship-challenged but mine isn't. Remember when we spent the holidays with my parents? You fit right in."

"If you say so." Sarah turned and snuggled against his shoulder, relaxing in his warmth. Mike was such a good guy, had a great dog and came from a happy family. Weird.

Trust Me

Sarah stepped into the cavernous elevator, dug in her pocket and pulled out a note with the name Doug Johansen, Floor 73, Columbia Tower. Doug, the male half of a couple on Kate's list, suggested that they meet in his office. Moments later the doors parted revealing a marble and mahogany reception area. Very nice, thought Sarah. She smoothed her gabardine lapels as she stepped out. A striking brunette, wearing a dark brown cashmere sweater and a delicate string of pearls, looked up from her desk and smiled. "May I help you?"

"Yes, I have an appointment with Doug Johansen." Sarah was glad she'd worn her new Anne Taylor pantsuit, extra make-up and polished boots.

The receptionist checked her computer screen and clicked the mouse, "Sarah Grady?"

"Yes."

"I'll tell him you're here." She picked up her phone set and punched two numbers. "Doug, Sarah Grady is here." She looked up at Sarah. "He'll see you now." She rose and led Sarah to an over-sized door, holding it open.

Match!

Sarah took a deep breath and walked in. Across the room a tall, lanky man appeared to be studying the view, deep in thought. Framed by a panorama of mountains across Puget Sound, he turned and approached her with an outstretched hand. "Welcome Sarah."

The door closed silently behind her. "Magnificent view," she said.

"Kept the blinds closed for years," he grinned. "I thought it interfered with my concentration."

Doug offered Sarah a chair at the conference table. She could see her reflection in the black walnut top. He sat across from her. "So. You want to know about the couples retreat. Jane and I attended it about five years ago."

"Yes my boyfriend, Mike, wants me to go with him. The two people I've already interviewed thought it was very helpful."

"Well, the weekend not only saved my marriage, it may have actually saved my life."

"How so?" Sarah asked. Then she stopped for moment. "I hope I'm not being too personal."

Doug leaned back in his chair. "Not at all. It's no secret that I was on the fast track to a heart attack. I ate, drank and slept my legal practice." He smiled at the memory. "On top of that I had a failing marriage. You see my mind was always on twenty things at once. If Jane wanted to talk, it interrupted important business."

"I understand. I'm a CPA and easily get lost in my work."

"There's a fine line between working hard and

Match!

workaholism. Financial achievement is pointless if it kills your marriage and ruins your health. Funny thing is, since I've slowed down and restructured my priorities, I've actually enjoyed more success. Business is still fantastic, my blood pressure is down and Jane and I share a life—not just a house."

"The retreat did all that for you?" Sarah was skeptical.

"No, we did it for ourselves. It wasn't a free ride. But the retreat gave us the tools to get started."

"What kind of tools?"

"Well, the information about feelings was really helpful. Until that time I had only two feelings: okay and mad. If Jane asked me how I felt, I'd say 'okay.' If she pressed for details, I'd get mad.

"At the retreat I started noticing sensations in my body. I discovered that the knot in my stomach and my heart racing were brought on by fear and anxiety. In the past when I had those feelings, without even realizing it, I'd get angry because it felt more powerful than fear. Is this making any sense?" Doug cocked his head.

"I think I'm following. Keep going, please."

"Well, anger wears thin after a while. You aggravate your blood pressure and stop feeling good about much of anything. You need to dig

If you have love in your life it can make up for a great many things you lack. If you don't have it, no matter what else there is, it's not enough.
ANN LANDERS

beneath the obvious; get to the feelings that the anger is covering."

"I don't know," Sarah said. "I never really understood about getting in touch with feelings. Why do I need to belabor them?"

"Yeah, I thought feelings were for girls and emergencies." They both laughed. "But if you don't know your real feelings, then you're unaware of what's motivating your actions—especially the bad behavior. Makes it hard to be in a relationship. I wanted career success but I also wanted my marriage."

"That's one of the amazing things about Mike," Sarah said. "He actually talks about his feelings. Me, I just shut down."

"Well, that weekend Jane and I did more talking, listening and kissing than we had since our honeymoon. And even the honeymoon was a stretch for me—the talking-listening part, that is."

"Are you still talking and listening?" Sarah asked.

"We forget at times. When I get stressed out and bring the office home, Jane calls me on it. She's pretty scrappy. It really helps that we can trust each other again."

"How do you rebuild trust?" asked Sarah.

"First let me tell you about how we destroyed it. Jane and I were masters at creating mistrust. Our house was a combat zone. What we didn't understand was that every time we snapped at each other, we paid for it by creating hurt and distance. I was belligerent and sarcastic, Jane was critical and demanding. Of course there are other ways to

Match!

wipe out trust like lying, infidelity, blaming."

"Yeah," said Sarah. "When I need more ideas I can always watch sitcoms."

"It was real easy for us to be jerks," Doug continued. "But to prevent our relationship from going to the divorce court, we had to learn how to build trust. We were clumsy at first, but eventually we learned to disagree without attacking. With effort we stopped the yelling and cruel remarks. We apologized when we screwed up."

"Sounds like a lot of work," said Sarah.

"It was. But we persisted. We took time to work things out through respectful discussions. We learned to enjoy each other again—do fun things together and visit like old friends. Eventually we developed new habits and a tremendous amount of trust. This insulates us during tough times."

Sarah nodded and said, "My parents only knew about attacking. I'm afraid I'll be the same way in a marriage."

"You can learn new ways to communicate, Sarah. I'm living proof of that."

As the conversation continued, Sarah was impressed by Doug's honesty and humility. The phone buzzed. Sarah glanced at the clock on his desk. They'd been talking almost an hour.

"Excuse me," Doug apologized, hanging up the phone. "Yet another fire that needs tending. Can I answer any more questions?"

"No. You've given me a lot to think about." She stood up from the table. "Thanks so much."

Match!

Doug escorted her back to the elevator. "Let me know if you decide to do the retreat," he waved. "Wish Jane and I had done it before we were married."

Sarah pegged Doug as confident and tough. His willingness to change surprised her. Maybe there is hope for me, she mused. As the elevator traveled down to the ground floor, she reviewed her week. She'd interviewed three people on Kate's list and scheduled appointments with three more: Jackie in a few days, Joe and Barb on Sunday afternoon. So far everyone had reported excellent results. Stepping outside, she drew her raincoat closer. Maybe attending the retreat wasn't such a bad idea after all.

The Blame Game

Thursday morning Sarah walked the two blocks from her condo to Starbucks swinging her insulated NPR coffee cup. She was meeting Jackie from Kate's couple number three. The rich aroma of fresh ground coffee beans greeted her as she entered the building. Glancing around she spotted a young woman wearing a red cardigan.

"Jackie?"

"Sarah?" A halo of brown curls framed a smiling bronze face, high cheekbones and huge ebony eyes.

"Be right back," Sarah said as she walked to the counter. "A grande caramel macchiato and a maple oat scone." She unfolded bills from her jeans pocket and then carried her plate and brimming coffee cup back to Jackie's table.

Match!

After an exchange of pleasantries Jackie explained how the retreat had helped her work through a major problem with her boyfriend, Ed.

"Exactly what about the weekend was most helpful?" asked Sarah.

"The really big bolt-out-of-the-blue for me was when Kate said that I had to give up blame and choose personal accountability. I blamed Ed for everything. Heck, if I stopped blaming Ed for things, I wouldn't have anything to talk about with my friends." Jackie took a sip of coffee.

"I'm kinda that way about blaming my parents," Sarah admitted, pushing crumbs into a pile on her napkin.

"Yeah, I blame my parents too. But lately it's been more fun to pick on Ed. Take our financial situation for example; when Ed and I started living together we agreed to split expenses 50/50. This worked for a few months when everything was shiny and new, but then I began to resent it."

"How so?"

"Well, Ed makes a lot more money than I do. After we moved in together, he still had cash in his wallet but I was just scraping by. I couldn't understand why he didn't offer to pay more of the expenses. I didn't say anything to him but I said plenty to my friends and family. After Kate's presentation on blame and accountability, I realized I was blaming Ed for not reading my mind."

"People aren't very good at that," Sarah smiled.

"At the retreat we discussed how we might work it out. We hit on sharing expenses based on a percentage of what

we each earned. It was a huge relief. Now whenever I feel victimy I remember to ask for what I want. Ooh, I sound like Barb."

"Barb?"

"Yeah, Barb was one of the assistants at the retreat. Do you know her?"

"Not yet," said Sarah, nibbling her scone. "But her husband, Joe, works with my boyfriend. We're meeting them later this week."

Jackie eyed Sarah's plate. "That looks good," she said, suddenly leaving the table. In a few minutes she returned with a mug and scone. "I learn by example."

Jackie continued to talk between bites. "Before we went to the retreat I was anxious to get married. Ed was reluctant. Now we're wondering whether or not to stay together. If we decide to split, I think we'll remain friends and that's way better than my past break-ups." Jackie glanced at her bare wrist. "Oops, do you have the time?"

Sarah checked her watch, "Wow, it's already 8:30. I didn't realize we'd been talking so long. I've got to get to the office."

"Me too." Jackie pushed back her chair and stood up, grabbing her cup and plate.

Sarah wiped the remaining crumbs into her napkin and thanked Jackie for her time. "The more I learn about the retreat," Sarah said, "the better it sounds."

"Well, I learned something this morning, too," said Jackie.

"What?"

Match!

"That I love scones!"

Sarah waved a cheery goodbye. But as she walked home, she couldn't stop thinking about Jackie's indecision over her future with Ed. Could the same thing happen with Mike?

Just Listen

Mike's Jeep bounced across the corrugated surface of the Aurora Bridge high above the ship canal. He turned into the Wallingford neighborhood. On a street of tidy, older homes, he pulled up in front of a craftsman cottage painted sparkling white with yellow shutters. Lavender grew between the slats of a white picket fence. Sarah got out of the car and immediately broke off a stem of lavender, crushing the dead blossom between her fingers. "Hmm, smell this, Mike." She passed it under his nose.

"Nice, but I'm a little busy right now," he huffed, struggling with 60 pounds of straining dog.

Sarah opened the gate into a dormant flower garden. A wisteria threaded through the porch railing. A stocky man wearing a bright red t-shirt stepped out through the doorway. Rex saw him and pulled harder on the leash. The man waved a dog biscuit in the air. "Here ya go Rexy!" he teased.

"Stop it Joe!" Mike laughed, grabbing at Rex's collar. Rex yanked free, tore across the yard and snatched the biscuit from Joe's hand. Then he took off around the corner of the house.

Match!

"That dog's gotta get out more," Joe called. "C'mon in. I need to check the oven."

"What a great place," said Sarah, stepping through the front door. "Smells like apple pie." And hopefully ice cream, she thought.

Barb rounded the side of the house taking the porch steps two at a time, Rex at her heels. She wiped her palms on her jeans and offered a perfectly manicured hand to Sarah. Then she hugged Mike, pulled off her baseball cap and shook out a mane of wavy auburn hair.

"Let's put the kids downstairs to play," she said, pushing the basement door open. "Mike, you and Sarah have a seat in the living room. Here Oscar!" A black lab rushed through the hallway with Rex in hot pursuit. The two dogs jostled down the steps as Barb closed the door. "Whew, those guys do love to see each other," she said.

Barb walked into the living room, tossed a log on the fire and then sat in a rocking chair across from Mike and Sarah. "It's good to finally meet you, Sarah. Mike tells us you're the best thing that's ever happened to him."

"Well, that's true," Sarah smiled.

"Thanks for taking time to talk to us," said Mike.

"No problem," said Barb. "The couples retreat is one of my favorite subjects."

"Mike's convinced it would be good for us," said Sarah, "and after listening to a lot of feedback about it, I'm inclined to agree with him."

"Whoa!" Mike fell back in the sofa. "This is news!"

"But I'd still like to hear about your experiences, Barb," said Sarah, grinning.

Match!

"Did I hear my name?" Joe walked in from the kitchen.

"No," said Barb.

"Well then why not?" He dropped into the overstuffed chair next to Barb, slinging his leg over the arm. "Barb and I went to the retreat because we had family problems."

"You mean *you* had family problems," said Barb. She turned to Sarah. "Joe's parents had a hard time accepting the fact that he wasn't moving back to the east coast to run the family business. They figured I was the main obstacle. They gave me the cold shoulder on the phone—just wanted to speak to sonny-boy." Barb tousled Joe's unruly, black hair.

Joe continued the story. "When Barb and I began talking about marriage, I wanted to elope. Barb wanted a big church wedding with family, friends and a reception at the Space Needle."

"Hey," said Barb, throwing her arms into the air, "If you're gonna do something, do it big."

"Barb wanted to invite everyone, my family included. I just couldn't get my head around sharing the day with my parents. They didn't approve of Barb and would've given me hell about it. Barb thought she could schmooz them but I knew the day would be ruined. Barb and I were at loggerheads."

Sarah knew about loggerheads.

"Then one of our friends told us about the couples retreat," said Barb.

"And we decided to go," Joe added.

Match!

"During the retreat we began to resolve things," said Barb. "Eventually we got married right here in front of the fireplace with the reception in the garden. His parents are learning to tolerate me, though they probably still blame me for taking him away from home."

"And away from a nice girl in the old neighborhood," Joe sighed, "who's so lonely without me."

"In your dreams," said Barb, smacking the back of his head. "At the time Joe wasn't sharing his feelings with me and I wasn't listening anyway. I was annoyed with him, which always makes me a little hard of hearing." Barb and Joe exchanged looks. "He was being pulled in two directions but after five years, it was time to get over it."

"So that's how we arrived at the retreat," said Joe. "We got along in every other way 95% of the time, if you didn't count Barb's temper fits and my silent periods."

"How did you get beyond the problem?" Mike asked. He took Sarah's hand but she was busy sniffing the fragrant apple scent wafting through the room.

"I think Sarah's distracted," said Joe. "Let's take a break." He stood up and pointed toward the kitchen. "To the pie!"

"Oh, thank goodness." Sarah jumped up. "Can I help?"

"Be my guest," said Joe.

Sarah practically fell over when she saw the source of that rich smell. It had to be the biggest pie she'd ever seen, complete with a flaky lattice crust.

Barb followed Joe and Sarah into the kitchen. "You're

Match!

not the first person to be bowled over by Joe's baking," she laughed, cutting generous slabs of pie and sliding them onto blue stoneware plates. "The family business is a chain of bakeries."

"Coffee?" Joe poured from the fresh brewed pot.

"Do you have half-and-half?" Sarah asked.

"No, but we have 1% milk."

"I'll just concentrate on the pie, thanks." Half-and-half was becoming an endangered species, thought Sarah.

As Joe and Barb headed for the dining room, Sarah remained in the kitchen, staring at the refrigerator. "Uh, I know this is rude," she called out, "but do you have any ice cream?"

"Do we have ice cream?" Barb marched back in and flung the freezer door wide. "Two shelves of designer ice cream and frozen soy dessert. Knock yourself out."

"I knew I liked you guys," said Sarah, foraging for the right flavor. She settled on vanilla bean. Everyone followed Sarah's example, scooping ice cream onto the steaming pie. Plates full, they gathered around the table in the cozy dining area.

"Okay," said Barb, putting down her fork. "You asked how we handled our problem. The answer is simple. First, Joe decided to share openly with me. He'd never been so honest. And second, I truly listened to him instead of just hearing my own agenda."

"Before, whenever I complained to Barb about my parents, she'd try to talk me out of it," said Joe.

"It'd never occurred to me to just listen," said Barb.

 Match!

"What a concept. When I just listened, things began to work out a little."

"How so?" Sarah asked, dabbing her mouth with the soft, blue cotton napkin. How could things begin to work out by just listening?

"When Barb tried to tear down my position," said Joe, "I automatically defended it. Then we went around and around like dogs chasing their tails. But when Barb shut up and listened, I could risk being more honest."

"And me too," mumbled Barb through a mouthful of warm pie and cold ice cream.

Joe continued, "If Barb tried to convince me that she was right, I got stubborn. When she was willing to listen, I loosened up. I actually shifted toward her position."

"Problems aren't solved in the mind states that create them," said Barb. "When Joe and I talked and listened to each other, we relaxed and discovered new possibilities. It wasn't always easy but our synergy held us together. We've been talking and listening ever since."

The evening ended too soon. Sarah and Mike exited amid promises of a repeat performance. Mike stuffed a reluctant Rex into the backseat.

"Hey, Joe," Sarah called out the window, "next time I'll bring the half and half."

Mike adjusted his seatbelt. "I'm stuffed," he muttered, finally starting the car.

Seek first to understand, then to be understood.
STEPHEN COVEY

 Match!

"Me too," Sarah groaned. "That Joe can bake a serious pie. Too bad your family doesn't own a bakery."

"You'd be in heaven. By the way, why didn't you tell me that you decided to go to the retreat?"

"It's a stretch for me, Mike. I guess it was hard to say the words, 'I'll go.'"

"It's gonna be good for us. You'll see."

Right, thought Sarah. As long as we don't decide to split up.

❖

Match!

PART II

Retreating

The retreat was being held at a conference center in the foothills of Washington's Cascade Mountain range. Sarah arranged the travel logistics meticulously. It helped reduce her anxiety. She took a half-day off from work, dropped Sophie at the Cat Clinic and headed east across Lake Washington on the Evergreen Point floating bridge. Pulling into Mike's driveway, she hoped he'd be packed and ready to hit the road at 3:30, right on schedule.

Mike stuck his head out the front door and yelled. "Be right there!" Then he disappeared back inside.

Ten minutes later she was still waiting in his driveway, fuming. What was he doing in there? Just as she was ready to physically drag him into the car, he popped out the front door.

"Finally!" she called from the car window. "What took you so long?"

"Couldn't find my gloves," he said.

 Match!

Tossing his backpack behind her, he fell into the seat and buckled up. "I made one last call to Dad about taking care of Rex."

"Okay you're forgiven," she growled. "But next time please be prompt."

Beyond the rush of city traffic Sarah began to unwind. She loved driving—hugging the curves as she accelerated. Too bad about the speed limit. She turned up the radio and Mike hummed along, tapping a quiet rhythm with his fingers.

"Great day for drive in the country," she said.

"No kidding," said Mike. "We should do this more often. Hey, I know! How about taking that trip to the Grand Canyon this summer? Rafting on the Colorado. Remember, I showed you the brochure?" He searched through his jacket pockets. "I've got it here somewhere. Six people to each boat, five boats in all, continuing education credits, thrills and adventure. Camping under the stars."

"Can I think about it?"

Mike turned off the radio and looked at her, "C'mon, you love the outdoors. It'll be a blast."

Sarah stared hard at the road.

"The deposit is due in April," he added.

"Just give me time to consider it, okay?" Sarah heard her voice rise.

"Oops!" Mike hid his face with his hands and then peered through his fingers. "Uhmmmmm, would that be a 'maybe'?"

Match!

Sarah smiled in spite of herself. "Why do I love you so much?"

Mike stretched out his legs and then dropped his arm over her shoulders. "I'm so darn cute."

"You're so darn something, that's for sure." They both relaxed, soothed by the quiet drone of the car. Trees flew by.

Sarah finally spoke. "I've been thinking about my conversations with the people on Kate's list. They talked about being distant, resentful or unhappy. Everyone had problems. Do you think we'll have those kinds of problems, Mike?"

"Sure, once in awhile," he said. "Put two people together and they'll find something to argue about." He massaged Sarah's neck as he spoke. "But if I wanted to spend my life with someone who agreed with everything I said, I'd stick with Rex. You help me consider another point of view. I like that."

"You do? Sometimes I feel like I'm a stick-in-the mud."

"Nah, you're just a nester." Mike gave her neck one final squeeze.

"Mike, look around you. Most people grow apart, getting more disagreeable through the years. I mean, we have a problem right now—this trip to the Grand Canyon. The truth is, I don't want to go."

"You don't? Why not?"

Sarah squeezed the steering wheel. "I don't mean to be a brat. It's just that I get three weeks of vacation. I'd like to take a week in December so we can go skiing and be with

the family. For the other two weeks I want to do something with just the two of us."

"I guess I could do the rafting trip alone," Mike said.

"You'd go rafting without me?" Sarah felt her cheeks flush.

"I thought you didn't want to go!"

Gravel crunched as Sarah turned into a wooded lane. A weathered sign pointed toward the left fork.

"It's...it's just that I'd miss you." She flashed on a picture of Mike at the campfire surrounded by a bevy of babes. Jealousy made her feel petty and insecure.

"Well, I'd miss you too, honey, but the trip earns twenty units toward my next pay raise."

Sarah pulled into a parking area and stopped next to a shiny blue van with Mountain View Lodge painted on its side. "I hate it when you appeal to my practical side," she sighed, staring at her hands. "It usually works." She turned to look at him. "I'm sorry. Sometimes I'm a big baby."

Mike gently tugged at her hair. "And sometimes I can be a little pushy." He tucked a loose strand behind her ear, turned her chin toward him and kissed her gently. "Okay?"

"Yeah," she smiled.

"Let's go inside."

They gathered their bags and strolled down a path of uneven stones. An afternoon mist hung over the rustic lodge, softening its corners. The windows were trimmed in white with the frames painted gray to match the silvered cedar roof. A porch stretched across the front of the building, wooden rocking chairs waiting at the rail. A

Match!

snow-capped peak dominated the vista.

"That's Mt. Pierson," said Mike. "Race you to the top."

"You're kidding." Sarah wasn't sure.

"Well there's a great hike to Pierson Falls. It's too late today but maybe another time."

"For now let's see if we can check-in. Then we can find a little café and get some dinner." Sarah was hungry, she was cold and she was nervous. All reasons to eat.

They walked up the steps to the front door. Sarah scanned the lobby interior, taking in the smell of smoky wood and waxed floors as her eyes adjusted to the dim light. Fir walls were yellowed with age. Heavy beams supported a cedar-planked ceiling and ornate wrought iron light fixtures cast a warm glow.

They followed voices to a spacious conference room overlooking the forest. A fire crackled in the massive rock fireplace. "Hi, are you here for the retreat?" called a woman from across the room.

"Yes we are," said Sarah. "I know we're a little early." The woman hurried toward them and extended her hand, "I'm Alicia and," she pointed to a burly man arranging the blue tweed stacking chairs, "that's my husband, Tom. We're assisting Kate and Jim." Alicia's sun-streaked brown hair skimmed her shoulders. Her hazel eyes warmed as Tom approached.

Mike stepped forward. "I'm Mike and this is Sarah."

"Glad you're here," Tom said.

Sarah noticed that Tom's hands were scarred and

Match!

callused, the hands of a man who knew hard work.

"We won't get started until 7:30 but let's check you in," said Tom.

Mike and Sarah visited with Tom and Alicia for a few minutes and then carried their bags to their room, waving off Tom's offer to help. Mike unlocked the door and swung it wide. "Gee I like this already," said Sarah, peeking in. "Just like summer camp." The tiny room contained two twin beds, a small end table and a lamp. Sarah turned up the electric heater and collapsed on the bed closest to the window. It squeaked in protest. Mike was busy searching through his backpack.

"What are you up to?" Sarah asked, raising herself up on one elbow.

Mike eyed her as he continued digging. Suddenly, "Tah-dah!" He snapped a red-checkered cloth into the air and draped it across the mattress.

Sarah sat up wide-eyed.

"Drum roll, please..." With a flourish, Mike produced two chicken-avocado sandwiches, followed by upscale paper plates, red cloth napkins, carrot sticks, Greek olives and two small bags of gourmet potato chips. He fumbled in the pack once more and retrieved two plastic wine glasses along with a bottle of sparkling cider. "Let the feast begin." He beamed at Sarah.

All the beautiful sentiments in the world weigh less than a single lovely action.
JAMES RUSSEL LOWELL

Match!

"It's fabulous, Mike!" Sarah grabbed a sandwich and settled on the floor next to the bed. "When did you do all this?"

"Last night," he said, pouring the cider. "The hard part was sneaking food from the fridge into the backpack while you were waiting in the driveway."

"Oh yeah." Sarah remembered her impatience. "That was dicey. I almost stormed in on you. And what about those gloves you couldn't find?"

"What gloves?"

They feasted on everything down to the last crumb. "That was the best," said Sarah, patting her stomach. "Thank you, Sir. I'm indeed a lucky woman."

"It warn't nothin'." Mike hung his head. Then he stretched out on the bed amid the plastic wrap and paper plates, thumbing through a dog-eared copy of *Hiking the Cascades*.

Sarah glanced at the clock, "Oh geez, it's almost 7:30. I only have a few minutes to get organized."

"Wait a minute." Mike held his book up so Sarah could see the picture. "Look, here's that Pierson Falls hike. Maybe we can do it Sunday before we head home."

"Let's just get through this retreat first." Sunday afternoon seemed a long way off. She blotted her lipstick and rushed out the door.

❖

Match!

Clear Intention

The meeting room bustled with activity. Chairs were now arranged in rows. A handful of people milled around the registration table while Alicia and Tom greeted latecomers. At 7:30 sharp Kate, who had been circulating among the couples, walked to the front of the room. "Glad everyone made it through the traffic. Will you all sit down so that we can get centered."

Sounds woo-woo, thought Sarah.

Kate began, "I want us to let go of the rush and busyness of getting here and relax into the possibilities and intention of the weekend. Rest your feet flat on the floor, dropping your shoulders, allowing your face to soften. Now, breathe in the refreshing mountain air and breathe out the obligations and concerns that may be clamoring for your attention. And in this state of relaxation I bring my attention to the perfect design for this weekend. Each of us has a gift to give and a gift to receive."

Sarah felt her apprehension dissolving as Kate's comforting words surrounded her.

"...we are here by divine appointment so I call this weekend good and very good...and so it is, amen."

"That was different," Sarah whispered in Mike's ear.

A silver haired man joined Kate at the front. I wonder if that's Jim, thought Sarah. Hmmm... A neatly trimmed beard and mustache; warm twinkling eyes set off by a blue plaid shirt and pressed khaki pants. A male version of Kate!

He introduced himself. "I'm Jim Wallace and you just

heard from my wife and partner, Kate. We're the facilitators and we'll be doing most of the presenting this weekend. Assisting with the retreat are Alicia Lopez and her husband, Tom Roberts. You'll be hearing from them tomorrow.

"We do have a few suggestions to help you get the most out of this weekend. Please turn off your cell phones, refrain from watching television and no newspapers or books. You are committing fully to your relationship for the duration of the retreat. Give it your undivided attention." He smiled. "I promise we'll keep you busy.

"Throughout the weekend we'll be sharing ideas through lectures and role-playing and providing time for you to practice new ways of interacting with each other. All of the exercises are done privately; many are written using the workbooks provided. We'll have a question and answer period tomorrow evening. Please write your questions on the slips of paper provided.

"We've been field-testing these ideas for almost twenty years in our own marriage and with couples whom we've coached. If you practice what you learn this weekend you'll dramatically improve your relationship. Over time you'll reap big rewards.

"Please turn to the Welcome page in your workbook and write your intention for the weekend. The question states, 'What do you want to get out of this retreat?' When you finish writing, exchange books with your partner and let him or her read what you wrote. We'll ring the chime when it's time to come back."

Match!

Sarah sat quietly wondering. Was her intention more than just appeasing Mike? She picked up her pen and wrote: I want to figure out how to have a happy marriage—*not* like my parents'. She sat back in her chair and reread the sentence. Yep, she decided, if I can get over that hurdle, the weekend will be well spent.

Mike nudged her. "You done?" They exchanged books.

Mike wrote: I want to convince Sarah to marry me.

"Two pieces of the same puzzle," Sarah whispered.

"I'll take that as a good omen," said Mike.

The chime rang and Jim walked back to the front of the room to continue talking.

"By clarifying your intention, you have focused your energy. By avoiding distractions such as reading and television, you'll maintain that focus. Clear intention combined with targeted actions can create profound results even in a short weekend. Working on your relationship is the most valuable project you could undertake. Take a peek at the statistics in your workbook and consider the alternatives."

Sarah's heart sank as she read the numbers. *(See Figure 1.)*

"Today it's commonplace for people to divorce more than once. Some experts argue that

---

It's estimated that in the United States of America 50% of all first marriages end in divorce, with some states being considerably higher, upwards to 66%. 50 to 75% of those who divorce, depending on age, will remarry. Of those who remarry, 50% or more of them will be divorced a second time within the first five years of the second marriages. Some estimate that almost half of all children are living in stepfamilies.
U.S. CENSUS AND OTHER DATA

Figure 1

the first marriage is only a practice run and should be expected to end. Others claim that single lifelong partnerships are things of the past. Because more people are living longer, serial marriages are desirable. Katie and I disagree with these opinions."

"Thank God," muttered Sarah.

"Divorce is one of the biggest epidemics going, an epidemic that is taking a huge spiritual, emotional, mental, physical and economic toll on couples, their children, their extended families and future generations. In most cases, it is less costly on every level to remain invested in your present marriage. In fact, shared memories and a lifetime of deepening intimacy and trust are priceless. Patience, flexibility, honesty, strength and courage are character traits developed through healthy long-term commitment. A lifelong relationship is not only doable, it is spiritually ideal."

Kate spoke up. "This is the relationship planet. We're born to interact with each other and it's about time we learned how to do it well."

Jim continued. "Kate and I specialize in facilitating relationship transformation. It's our mission to help couples stay together and bless the world in the process. You are choosing to be part of this healing wave of change. Congratulations—let's get to it!"

Relationship Evolution

Kate took over, "Tonight I'm going to introduce the concept of relationship evolution. Your relationship goes

through distinctive phases of growth and development. The better you understand these phases, the better you'll navigate through them and reap the rewards they offer.

"The initial phase of a relationship is romance. You meet, fall in love and are enchanted by each other. We all know about romance because it's well represented in the media and many people believe that it epitomizes the perfect relationship. But romance always evolves into the second phase, turbulence. This is a developmental period that requires you to work through your differences and conflicts. Turbulence can periodically reassert itself throughout the lifetime of your relationship, however its most aggressive manifestation typically occurs after romance. How well you handle turbulence determines the ultimate form into which your relationship evolves: synergistic, parallel, volatile or separated. You'll find a diagram in your workbook illustrating this progression." *(See Figure 2.)*

Kate propped a copy of the diagram on the easel at the front of the room. "The information and exercises that we present this weekend are all aimed at helping you grow your relationship from romance through turbulence and into a synergistic union—a mature, creative, lifelong partnership. But I'd like to briefly touch on three of the less desirable outcomes: parallel, volatile and separated. You may recognize aspects of them in your own partnership or extended family.

"In the parallel relationship a couple stops attempting to resolve problems and settles into an apathetic truce.

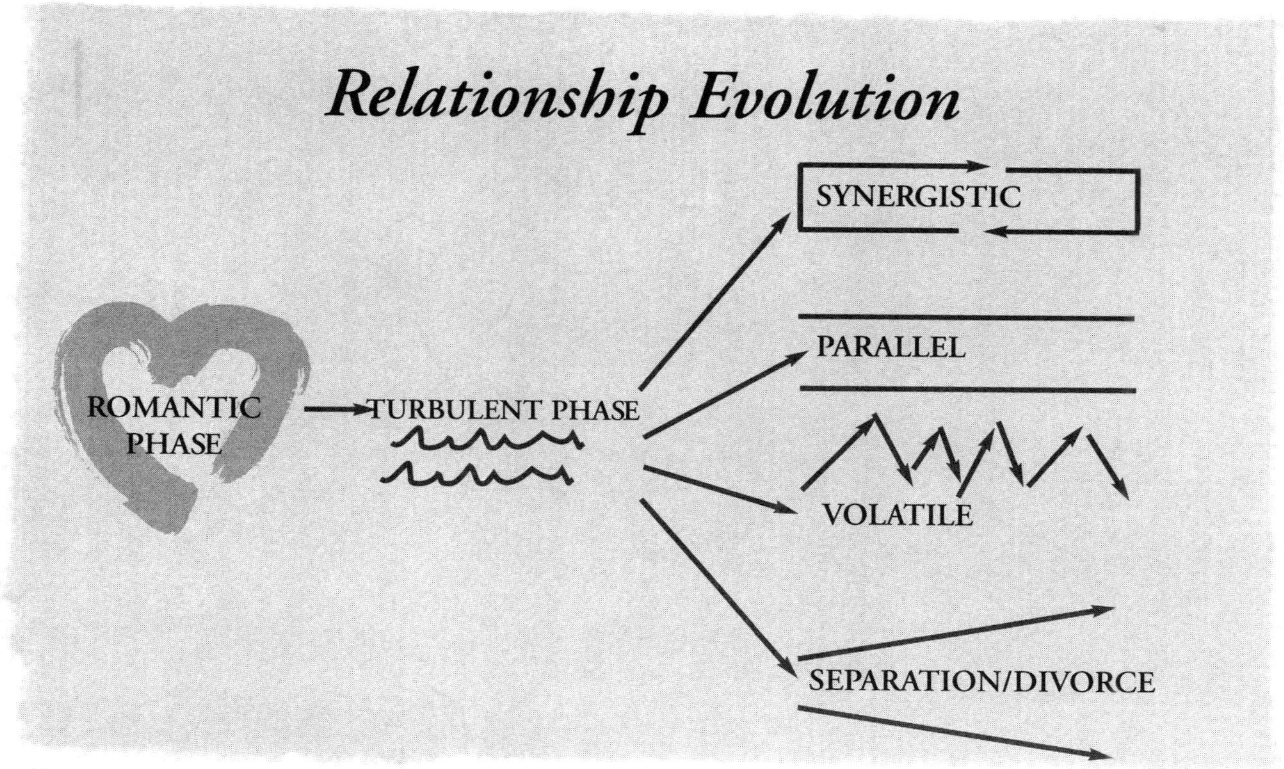
Relationship Evolution
ROMANTIC PHASE
TURBULENT PHASE
SYNERGISTIC
PARALLEL
VOLATILE
SEPARATION/DIVORCE

Figure 2

Match!

They may share a house and children but there is no warmth or caring between them. Extramarital affairs may be tolerated, even encouraged. Their response to a problem is: It's your life; you handle it. This union could be described as cold and distant."

Hmm…thought Sarah, that might describe my brother's marriages.

"In the volatile relationship the couple connects through conflict, sometimes loud and blatant, others times subtle and hidden. Often one partner claims superiority over their mate. The home is an armed camp of one-upmanship, hot and tense. Their response to a problem is: It's your fault."

Mike leaned over and whispered, "Does that sound familiar?" Sarah raised her eyebrows and nodded—her parents.

"Threats, criticism, sarcasm, depression and hurt feelings are common in the volatile relationship," said Kate. "Cycles of emotional turmoil are often followed by passionate reconciliation, especially when physical abuse is present." *(See Figure 3.)*

Sarah noticed silence in the room. It seemed like everyone related in some way to Kate's words. What a downer.

"These descriptions are simplified worst-case scenarios but relationships are seldom

Note: If you or your children are being physically abused or threatened, get help and get safe. Most cities have Crisis Services listed in the white pages of the phone book with a 24-hour hotline. The number for the national hotline for domestic violence is **1-800-799-SAFE**.

Figure 3

uncomplicated," said Kate. "You may be inclined toward volatile outbursts with a few aspects of parallel thrown in. Or you and your partner could be sliding into parallel lifestyles without realizing it. There are countless pressures influencing the evolutionary direction of your relationship.

"Occasionally divorce is the only answer. However, often times divorce is the result of poor decisions due to immaturity, inability and fear.

- Immaturity manifests as a lack of foresight and vision. We don't know what a truly adult, synergistic relationship looks like. We don't know what's possible.
- Inability manifests as a lack of communication skill. Even if we communicated well during romance, we don't know how to carry it through turbulence. We need role models and practice.
- Fear manifests as being overwhelmed by the task at hand. When romance fades, we try to rekindle the past. Because we can't go backward, we flounder, looking for quick fixes, grasping at straws, often giving up entirely.

"If any of this sounds too familiar, try not to worry. You're here at the retreat to learn healthy, respectful, loving and skillful ways to reconnect. Even if you're contemplating divorce, you can still make course corrections. Happily-ever-after is still possible."

Then Jim began speaking. "And what does happily-

ever-after look like? It is our personal favorite, the synergistic relationship. This is a partnership between equals. In a synergistic association, roles are flexible. No role is one-up or one-down. Challenges can still occur but the dominant mind set is positive, loving and supportive. Blame is a waste of energy. No one threatens to leave the marriage. Synergistic couples believe in the sanctity of their union. Their response to a problem is: We'll overcome this together."

"At this point romance is no longer a phase, it's a way of life," said Kate

Sign me up for that one, thought Sarah. She reached over and squeezed Mike's hand.

Vows

"Jim wasn't the first person I'd been in love with," Kate continued. "I had other relationships but alas, the state of being-in-love always ended. I wondered why things were terrific in the beginning and bad at the end. I failed to notice that I was terrific in the beginning and bad at the end. Instead of simply blaming my partner, I needed to unabashedly look at how I contributed to the downfall. I asked myself, what really happened and how can I do better?"

Jim piped in, "That's the million dollar question."

"We think we've found some answers to help you do better this time," said Kate. "Please turn to the page in your workbook titled Partnership Vows."

PARTNERSHIP VOWS:

I COMMIT fully to our relationship.
I LISTEN with an open heart and open mind.
I SPEAK honestly, with kindness and respect.
I NURTURE our relationship in thought and deed.

"The vows contain four simple practices that lead to a lasting, more fulfilling relationship. You will find that they reflect the characteristic behaviors of the romantic phase:

- COMMIT: You can't imagine life without your beloved. You're not looking for someone better or a way out.
- LISTEN: You listen with rapt attention. Your beloved is fascinating, someone you can learn from.
- SPEAK: When you speak to your beloved, you're honest and kind. You're cooperative, considerate and gracious.
- NURTURE: You feed your union by focusing on what is highest and best about your beloved. You share your love through affection and attention.

"The path from romance into synergy is embodied by the Partnership Vows. When the vows are forgotten or ignored, the relationship often cannot survive turbulence. When the vows are practiced with consistency and sincerity, the relationship blossoms."

Mike leaned over to Sarah. "This seems pretty obvious," he whispered. "If I'm in love, I should want to do these things naturally."

Match!

Kate continued. "Romance is like a short-term spiritual experience. God's grace lifts you above and beyond your ordinary self. People in love will behave beautifully at first. But after the newness wears off, it's easy to get lazy. A lifelong relationship takes effort. You're not only remembering why you fell in the love in the first place, but you're also attempting to find new ways of expressing it. This takes energy and intention, especially during turbulence."

"Hence the vows," whispered Mike, "for the relationship-challenged."

"I'm thankful for them because I'll forget," said Sarah. "Especially when I'm crabby or tired." Who knows, she thought, they might actually work.

"Practicing the vows isn't always easy," said Kate. "Simple things, no matter how important, can quickly be undervalued or ignored. However, if you use these vows as a compass, you'll help confine conflict to current circumstances and maintain a foundation of trust. The vows are a code of ethics that help you walk the spiritual path of love.

"The first vow is about commitment. Each of you is demonstrating commitment to your relationship by being here this weekend. Let's focus that commitment by agreeing to abide by the vows for the duration of the weekend. I'd like you to turn your chairs so that you're facing your partner, look into your partner's eyes and repeat the vows after me. Remember, at this point we're only asking you to practice these vows for the next 48 hours."

Match!

Love Letters

Jim stepped forward and gave Kate a quick squeeze. "Thanks Katie." He smiled at the group. "Your partner has many fine qualities and traits that you admire. These could include kindness, courage, tenacity and so forth. Please write a love letter describing these qualities and include specific examples. If you're not specific, your partner may not believe you."

Sarah remembered the first time she saw Mike. She was attending a ski club meeting when she spotted a guy standing by the door. Talk about love at first sight. He was about 6 feet tall, maybe 160 pounds and did those jeans ever fit. By the end of the evening they'd made a date to walk around Green Lake. Sarah leaned over and gave Mike a little kiss on the cheek.

"What was that for?" he asked.

"Just for being such a hottie," she winked.

Jim continued to describe the exercise. "Don't make this hard. If you run out of things to say then start a new sentence with the words, 'I also admire...' The purpose of this exercise is to reconnect with the loving spirit underlying your relationship. We'll chime when the writing time is over. You'll then take turns reading your letters to each other."

Sarah eyes sparkled as she read her love letter to Mike. When she finished, he took her face in his hands and kissed her. "Thank you," he said. "I hope I can live up to all those words."

Match!

"You already have," said Sarah. "Now you read to me."

Mike read, "The first time we met I was drawn to your quiet intensity and your physical beauty. Your intelligence and grace continue to inspire me. You are so strong and full of surprises. I value your opinion because I know you'll never just go along. You're definitely your own person. All I know is that you are the love of my life."

"Ooh, I could listen to this all the time," crooned Sarah. Other couples sat with their heads close together, voices soft. When the exercise was over, Sarah took Mike's hand, turned it palm up and kissed it.

"I feel stupid in love," she said.

Jim chimed and scanned the assemblage. "Doesn't it feel good to focus on the things you appreciate about your partner? On this sublime note we'll end our evening. After breakfast tomorrow we'll tackle the turbulent phase. Then you'll do a self-evaluation regarding those pesky differences, practice gracious listening, become more mindful about your everyday interactions and, if that's not enough, learn to walk the heart path to a happier and healthier relationship. Good night everyone."

Mike stood up. "May I carry your book?"

"I guess so. And then how'd you like to rearrange the furniture? Maybe push those beds together?" Sarah grabbed the front of Mike's shirt and pulled him toward her.

Turbulence

Sarah woke up with a start. It was 8:10; breakfast was served at 8:00. Mike's bed was empty. Last night he'd

Match!

mentioned a morning walk. She quickly freshened up, ran a brush through her hair, threw on jeans and a sweater and waited for him to return. After ten minutes of tapping her fingers, she left for the dining room. There she spotted Mike seated and deep into a conversation with Kate. She strode over to him, forcing a smile.

"Hi honey," he said, getting to his feet and pulling out a chair.

Sarah remained standing. "I thought you'd come back to the room," she whispered.

"Oh gosh. Did I say I was coming back to the room?"

"No."

"Did you ask me to come back to the room?"

"Uh, no. But you could have left me a note."

"I'm sorry I wasn't clear. But hey, tomorrow morning I'll know." Mike grinned.

Sarah smiled back at him. "I think we just learned something about communication: Don't assume."

Sarah headed for the buffet table. She stood weighing her options: Pancakes or oatmeal with fruit? She returned with her tray, licked syrup off her fingers and dug in. As people finished eating the room grew loud with conversation. Sarah strained to understand the woman to her left. She looked to be about Sarah's age.

"I'm Meagan and this is my husband, Jake."

"Pleased to meet you," mumbled Sarah, swallowing the last bite of her stack. "How are you liking the retreat?"

"I think it's great," gushed Meagan.

"How about you, Jake?" Sarah asked. His silence intrigued her.

 Match!

"The jury's still out," he muttered pushing back from the table. "Might as well get ready for the next round," he said, heading off for the conference room.

"Guess I'd better catch-up," said Meagan, rising. She grabbed both plates and scurried away.

Hmm...not one of those happy couples, thought Sarah.

Mike leaned over. "Ready for action?" he asked.

Sarah yawned as they walked to the meeting room. Maybe three pancakes had been too many. Settled in her seat she gazed out the window at the glistening ferns, shifting to stay awake.

At the front of the room, Kate and Jim perched on stools next to each other. Sarah wondered if she and Mike would look like that in 25 years? She'd be a lot taller of course. Whoa—there she was lost in the future. She laughed out loud and covered her mouth.

Mike nudged her. "What?"

"I'm just indulging my rich fantasy life." She pointed toward Kate. "Shush...we're missing something."

"Good morning," Kate began. "As promised we're going to talk about the phase that comes hot on the heels of romance." Kate paused and her eyes widened. "Turbulence."

Sarah thought this would be a great moment for a clap of thunder.

"You've probably heard this term used by airline pilots. But just like on the airliner, you can rise above it. If the romantic phase represents enchantment, the turbulent phase represents disenchantment. The new you wears off

·57·

Match!

and the old you takes over. Those charming quirks in your partner become annoying. Jim and I will share a few communication problems we encountered when our realities collided during the turbulent phase of our relationship." She looked at Jim.

"Katie had an artistic, tidy home when we met," explained Jim. "She loved to cook, garden and entertain. By contrast, I enjoyed a rather basic lifestyle, drank lots of pop and shared custody of my 13-year-old son, Ben. Ben and I truly intended to recycle our empty soda bottles but they hadn't filled up the dining room yet."

Kate cut in. "I thought it was refreshing how he didn't spend time worrying about housework; he was having too much fun. I admired his relaxed attitude."

Jim continued. "We had very different approaches to taking care of the house. For several months we worked around each other but eventually we began to experience turbulence. Kate and I will role-play one small example:

Kate: Jim, I thought you and Ben agreed to empty the trash. You're not doing it and I'm angry.
Jim: We agreed to empty it but I swear the trashcan is never full.
Kate: That's because you guys never empty it. I go crazy and take it out.
Jim: Okay, well that would explain why it's never full.
Kate: What are you talking about? It gets full, sometimes for a whole day. This has been going on for weeks.
Jim: I never see it full. Never!

Match!

Kate: Does the trashcan magically fill whenever I walk by and then magically empty whenever you're here?

Jim broke out of character to speak to the group. "Katie was angry for weeks about the trash not being emptied but she never said a word. Instead she became a silent martyr and emptied the trash herself. Understandably her resentment grew."

I do that, thought Sarah. I'm so afraid of sounding like my mom that I don't ask for what I want. I just stuff things. When I blow up, I come off huffy and heavy-handed.

"Katie wasn't living up to her vow about speaking honestly. She wasn't asking for what she wanted. By emptying the trash herself, she relieved us of the obligation to keep up our end of the bargain."

Kate chimed in. "I had quality assurance because I did it myself. But I also resented it because Jim wasn't doing his part."

"It's hard to live up to Katie's standards," said Jim, grinning at Kate.

"True," said Kate. "So the question was, did I want to control or did I want to share the load? Thankfully Jim's pretty good natured about my control issues..." she nudged him, "...most of the time."

"Okay, so let's talk trash again," said Jim. "As the scene unfolds, we're on the back porch looking into the trashcan which is filled to about four inches below the top."

Match!

Kate: It's full.

Jim: It's not full.

Kate: So Jim, what would it take for you to describe this trashcan as full?

Jim: A full trashcan is piled up to the top. All the trash should just fit into the bag when I pull it out of the trashcan. It's never been that full since we've lived here so I never thought it needed to be emptied.

Kate: That explains a lot.

Jim: Sure does.

Kate: Do you think you'd be willing to empty it when it was, say three or four inches below the rim?

Jim: For you, sure.

Jim broke out of character again. "Katie was hot when the conversation began and I knew I hadn't been emptying the trash." Jim paused. "But honest to God, it was never full."

"Oh sure..." Kate said.

"We had different definitions for a full trashcan and this created a perception gap. Once we understood each other's perceptions, we worked it out. I remembered to empty it most of the time. Katie still occasionally emptied it when it was well below four inches. Sometimes I went wild and emptied it when it seemed roomy, just to make her day."

Match!

Preference and Style Differences

Jim continued to talk about relationship turbulence. "The turbulent phase brings the discovery that you and your partner are not always on the same page. Many of you know all too well some of your partner's differences."

A few people chuckled.

"Your differences don't have to be a point of contention when you can understand and appreciate where your partner is coming from. This is when many couples get stuck—they don't realize that they can respect their partner's point of reference without compromising their personal beliefs. They can collaborate. The partner can then extend the same courtesy.

"Of course, some differences do cause more friction than others; discovering a collaborative solution can take effort. You may need to confront the situation several times. But as long as the vows serve as your communication ground rules, the discussion will remain honest, safe, enlightening and ultimately productive. Collaborative solutions reveal themselves when you allow the time and space to consider new possibilities. It's great to discover that your world has more options than you originally imagined. But you can't see these options as long as you remain attached to blame and escalating dissonance.

"For example, Katie loves to garden and wants the yard to look perfectly groomed. I hate yard work. After extensive diplomatic negotiations we agreed that she'd do the gardening she enjoyed and we'd pay someone else to do

the rest. If she insisted that I garden, we'd have created conflict. Instead, we both got what we wanted."

"Basic traits aren't going to change," said Kate, "and expecting them to do so is a no-win situation. The I'm-right-your-wrong mentality generates only pain and distance. It won't work. The keys to resolving conflict are consideration, collaboration and appreciation."

"Let's find some ways that you and your partner differ," said Jim. "Open your workbook to the section on differences. By differences, we mean preferences, temperament and personality styles that are dissimilar. We have a list of fifteen common differences. I'll go over the instructions before you begin. When we call time you can compare notes. *(See Figure 4.)*

"Try to keep your perspective positive. Talk about the strengths that your differences can bring to the relationship and how you balance each other. Talk about the benefits of understanding each other's perspective. I'm not telling you to ignore the problems that they create, but I'm suggesting that you approach them with an uplifted point of view. Remember, your partner's preference or style isn't wrong—it's just different."

Sarah leaned towards Mike, reading his choices. Their differences were alarming: he was messy, she was tidy; he was process-oriented, she was results-oriented; he was recharged by people and activity, she was recharged by solitude and quiet; he was carefree and intuitive while she was serious and did the research. And if that wasn't enough, she scribbled at the bottom of the page that she

Preferences and Styles Differences

Compare columns A and B in each row against your own behavior and circle the number that most closely matches you. EXAMPLE: In the first row: if you are very Tidy, circle the '5' closest to Tidy. If you are moderately tidy, circle '1' or '2' on the Tidy side. If you are extremely messy, circle the '5' closest to Messy. If you are between the two extremes, circle '0'.

Messy	5	4	3	2	1	0	1	2	3	4	5	Tidy
Process Oriented	5	4	3	2	1	0	1	2	3	4	5	Results Oriented
Recharged by People/Activity	5	4	3	2	1	0	1	2	3	4	5	Recharge by Solitude/Quiet
Likes to Debate Things	5	4	3	2	1	0	1	2	3	4	5	Hates to Debate Things
Spontaneous, Likes Change	5	4	3	2	1	0	1	2	3	4	5	A Planner, Likes Stability
Spender	5	4	3	2	1	0	1	2	3	4	5	Saver
Wants Children	5	4	3	2	1	0	1	2	3	4	5	Doesn't Want Children
Expresses Feelings	5	4	3	2	1	0	1	2	3	4	5	Stuffs Feelings
Warm, Outgoing	5	4	3	2	1	0	1	2	3	4	5	Reserved, Aloof
Night Person	5	4	3	2	1	0	1	2	3	4	5	Morning Person
High Sex Drive	5	4	3	2	1	0	1	2	3	4	5	Low Sex Drive
Gullible	5	4	3	2	1	0	1	2	3	4	5	Skeptical
Carefree	5	4	3	2	1	0	1	2	3	4	5	Serious
Goes With Intuition	5	4	3	2	1	0	1	2	3	4	5	Does the Research
Know What I Feel	5	4	3	2	1	0	1	2	3	4	5	Know What I Think

Figure 4

was a cat person while he was a dog person. When time was called, Sarah's stomach hurt.

"Hey," Mike protested. "You like ol' Rex."

"Sure, he's okay as a stepdog but who'd buy one? All that walking and scooping. Yuk."

"You scoop in a litter-box."

"Trust me, it's not the same."

Sarah considered the list carefully. How would it be to live with someone who was so different? How could a relationship survive? She decided to check it out. "Hey, do you feel upset when I want to stay at home and you want us to go out with your buddies?"

"Well, I do enjoy going out with friends."

"I work with so many people all week that by Friday night I crave solitude," Sarah countered.

"From my perspective," said Mike, "being with a bunch of friends, laughing and goofing around blows off a lot of stress."

Sarah closed her eyes. I wonder how we'll work through this? The thought of Jackie and Ed splitting up briefly crossed her mind.

"You okay?" asked Mike.

"Yeah, just thinking…"

Jim called them back. "Now you've talked about some of your differences. I didn't see any big fights break out." Jim paused and smiled. A few people looked worried.

"Katie's neat as a pin, I'm a slob," said Jim. "This difference will cause perpetual conflict if we let it. We minimize the friction by being considerate and keeping our

 Match!

vows at the forefront. I've also learned to appreciate and enjoy the ambience of being neat."

"And I've become more relaxed," said Kate. "There are days I don't even make the bed. I feel so wild and free."

Jim reached over and gave Kate a squeeze. "You saw Katie and me work through the trashcan thing. We didn't do it perfectly and you don't have to either. We raised our voices a little and Katie got a tad sarcastic, but all in all we did pretty well. It's normal to have conflict, to be angry, as long as you move through it while staying essentially connected and respectful."

We need not think alike to love alike.
FRANCIS DAVID

Sarah looked around the room. Surely she wasn't the only person who thought staying connected and being in conflict was an oxymoron.

Jim continued. "It can be a challenge to remain connected when you're angry. Our rule of thumb is, if we're too angry to sit next to each other and be civilized, then we're not ready to deal with the situation. We need a time-out, a cooling off period. We never discuss a problem when we're overwhelmed or too reactive to think clearly."

Jim formed the letter T with his hands. "This is a time-out symbol. It means that the ball's out of play. The game is called off until the players

Match!

thoroughly calm down." Jim looked at Kate. "We don't have time-outs anymore, do we?"

"Not many." She cocked her head and winked.

"Slamming the door is *not* a good way to initiate a time-out. You're not looking to fuel the anger. Time-outs should be a shared decision between the two of you. In our case, Katie goes walking and I pick up my favorite magazine. We haven't created a bigger emotional and mental gulf by continuing to fight. We still feel connected even though we're apart.

"Once you cool off and are ready to talk about the problem, it's important to try to sit facing each other. You'll be more likely to emotionally connect. If necessary, start with the chairs several feet apart and then move closer in increments. If you can't face each other, you may not be ready to talk yet. Once you're facing each other, try to stay physically close. Give a gentle touch, a hand squeeze. This breaks the habit of creating distance when you disagree."

Sarah gazed outside for a moment. It seemed plausible. But staying physically close during a disagreement, that could be tricky. She much preferred distance.

"In our trashcan scenario," said Jim, "we ended with a resolution. But some differences create problems that can become entrenched. Anger and accusations harden the problem. You may need to discuss it many times. It can be frustrating and even scary. But each time you talk about it honestly, with kindness and respect; each time you listen with an open heart, the problem softens. Be tenacious. Don't give up. Repeated respectful communication soaks

the problem in warmth and like rice stuck to the rice cooker, the problem eventually loosens and floats away. Your differences may remain but they're no longer a concern.

"Every time you mindfully move through challenges together you learn more about yourself, your partner and life. You become wiser, more resilient and mature. Being in conflict and still being kind and caring is the spiritual path of relationship. It builds character and creates intimacy. It's one way God speaks through partnership."

Bingo! Sarah scribbled notes to herself. Even though Jim and Kate raised their voices, they didn't get mean-spirited.

Kate continued. "The turbulent phase is graduate school for lovers, the time to build trust, learn how to work through problems and conflicts together and get to know each other at depth. This is when the rewards of a long-term, committed relationship begin to accumulate. If you find yourself in a parallel relationship, a volatile relationship or separated from each other, you can safely assume that you flunked out of graduate school. But that's okay. Lots of people do. You get another opportunity starting this weekend.

"In your workbook there's a page titled Hot Topics. We've provided this page for you to list topics you'd like to discuss with your partner. Maybe it's a situation that's unresolved or something that you'd like to discuss before it becomes a problem. Maybe it's a goal you're afraid to share. You may not be ready to reveal it yet. However, by writing

Match!

it in your notebook, you're declaring that at some point you'll collaborate on the issue. Respectful dialogue incubates the topic as it evolves into a solution, a non-issue or a shared vision. Please take time before the break to jot down some topics. As the weekend progresses and things come up, please add them to the list. It will also be a resource for an exercise we'll be introducing this afternoon."

Sarah knew exactly what she wanted to list: Fear of marriage and the Grand Canyon trip.

Gracious Listening

"We're now going to move into some skill building exercises that will help you express your anger and hurt in honest, yet respectful ways," said Kate.

Something that's totally lacking in my family, thought Sarah, something I need to practice.

"Working with turbulence demands effective communication skills. Perhaps the most overlooked and under appreciated of these is gracious listening. Gracious listening is embodied in the partnership vow: I listen with an open heart and open mind. When you're open hearted, you allow yourself to be touched emotionally by what your partner is communicating. This unites you. When you're open minded, you're willing to be influenced by the opinions and wisdom of your mate. This helps you grow. Gracious listening creates a sacred circle of trust where you are each free to share your cherished dreams as well as your

deepest fears. Intimacy and understanding flourish. As you will note on The Art of Gracious Listening, there are many benefits. *(See Figure 5.)*

"This list is a self-evaluation exercise. Circle the statements that best typify your listening style. For example, I'm personally challenged by number six; listening for understanding, not precision. I tend to take the low road by pointing out errors in picky facts. Shall we demonstrate, Jim?"

"It would be my pleasure, Katie." Jim stood next to Kate and began the scenario:

Jim: I'm going down to Canada tomorrow and...
Kate: Up to Canada.
Jim: What?
Kate: You're going up to Canada.
Jim: That's what I said. I'm going up to Canada tomorrow.
Kate: No, you said you were going down to Canada.
Jim: Forget it! *Jim turns his back on Kate and folds his arms.*

Kate laughed and turned to the group. "This really stops the flow of the conversation."

"It's annoying," said Jim, "and she used to do that all the time."

"I apologize, Jim. I'm trying to stop." Kate gave him a big smile and patted his arm. "This is a steep learning curve, but you get credit for little steps. The first step is

The Art of Gracious Listening
❖

BENEFITS

•A deeper connection with and understanding of your partner

•A delightful improvement in the atmosphere of your home

•A release of vital energy and enthusiasm formerly locked in conflict

•An ability to explore collaborative solutions with your partner

• A rewarding experience of self-discovery through deep and honest sharing

HIGH ROAD	LOW ROAD
1. Sit next to each other, close enough to touch.	1. Stand across the room with arms folded.
2. Listen to understand and connect.	2. Listen to better defend your position.
3. Listen until your partner is through talking.	3. Interrupt, try to fix it, give advice.
4. Ask clarifying questions and/or paraphrase.	4. Jump to conclusions, make assumptions.
5. Listen with an open heart and open mind.	5. Let defensive feelings close you off.
6. Listen for understanding, not precision.	6. Correct grammar or picky facts.
7. Be fully present with, and attentive to partner.	7. Show impatience, let your mind wander.
8. Listen in the here and now.	8. Interpret based on past experiences.

Figure 5

Match!

simply noticing when you say or do something that creates distance rather than closeness. Do you want to be right, or do you want to be happy?

"In our scenario," Kate said, "Jim folded his arms and turned away from me—my remarks created distance. I noticed and I apologized for it. As I continue to awaken, I hope I'll have less of an urge to correct picky facts. In any case, being close to Jim is more important.

"Now it's time to evaluate yourself. When you're through, take turns with your partner talking about any insights you gained. See if you can graciously listen to what your partner has to say. We'll chime when it's time to come back."

Sarah discovered that she'd circled far more on the low road side of the equation. I have a long way to go, she thought, but I'm giving myself credit for baby steps; for being awake enough to recognize listening habits that need to change.

Jim chimed and called everyone back together. "As you move through the exercises this weekend and later work through conflicts at home, remember first and foremost to listen graciously. It is the bedrock upon which all skillful communication rests."

Connections or Collisions

As Sarah and Mike readied themselves for the next session, they noticed Kate curled up in an overstuffed chair by the fireplace, apparently asleep. "You can tell she's been doing

this awhile and knows how to catch a few z's when she can," Mike observed.

"Kate and Jim seemed pretty relaxed all right," Sarah agreed. "I like the easy way they work together."

"They've had a lot of practice. It's something for us to look forward to."

Typical Mike, thought Sarah. But she found herself hopeful in spite of her fears. Was she actually becoming optimistic about their future together?

Jim motioned to the couples to return to their seats and Kate joined him at the front. "We're going to discuss being awake," she said, covering her mouth and yawning.

Jim glanced at Kate and raised an eyebrow. "You were saying?"

Kate shrugged her shoulders. "Hey, I need to practice waking up as much as any of you." She took a sip of tea. "Think about how much of your life you spend on autopilot. I bet you've driven to a destination without remembering the details of getting there." People smiled in recognition. "How often have you performed habitual tasks without thinking about them?" Heads nodded. "There's nothing inherently wrong with living on autopilot. In many cases it helps us navigate the complexities of our lives. The problem is that we get used to being unconscious and carry it into places where it doesn't belong. Are there situations with your mate when your hackles are up before a word is spoken? Sadly, as relationships mature, many people start responding on autopilot. They hear what they've heard in the past. They

Match!

expect the same old behavior and react to it before it's occurred." Kate paused to let the concepts sink in.

"When the Buddha was asked, 'Who are you?' he answered, 'I am awake.' Being awake is a state of conscious awareness. When you're awake, you can choose your response to life based on what's happening now, rather than your personal history or imagined future. When you and your partner relate from a state of conscious awareness, you evolve as individuals and the relationship ripens and deepens.

"The spiritual path of relationship is about waking up together and creating a loving reality. You become a wiser, healthier, happier and more interesting person and so does your mate. We call this the heart path, the high road. The unconscious path is the low road. By taking the low road you are choosing a lifetime of faultfinding, upset, sadness and stagnation.

"I want you to close your eyes and think about a typical weekday in your home. Start first thing in the morning. What would be a familiar first exchange between you? Let your mind drift through the morning, going off to work, coming home, the evening together. In all of those hundreds of little opportunities you have to join with each other, do you generally take the high road or the low road? You can open your eyes.

"It's so easy to fall into the habit of taking the low road in your ordinary, moment-by-moment interactions. Low road behaviors include being critical, contemptuous, bullying, hostile, defensive, disinterested, sullen or silent.

Match!

I'm sure you can think of more. All these behaviors are extremely hazardous to your relationship; they close your heart and hurt. Tom Roberts and Alicia Lopez, our registrars, will role-play one of their personal low road moments. Tom and Alicia are in our facilitator-training program."

Tom began. "If you want to get just one thing out of the weekend, this might be it—guard against those low road moments. Here's how it worked for us: Alicia came home from a hard day at work to find me sitting in front of the computer playing a game."

Tom sat down and pretended to type while Alicia walked up behind him:

Alicia: Hi, honey.
Tom: *Continues playing game.*
Alicia: I had a horrible day.
Tom: Mmm. *Tom continues playing the computer game.*
Alicia: Your stupid computer game is more important than me?
Tom: *Sighs and rolls his eyes. He gets up from computer and walks over to Alicia.* I'm here now. Whaddaya want?
Alicia: I don't want anything. You don't care!
Tom: You're right!

Alicia turned to the group. "I tried to engage Tom, get him to talk to me but ended up taking the low road and attacked him for ignoring me."

Match!

"And I wanted to keep playing my game so I purposely ignored her," said Tom. "I knew she'd eventually attack because it's a familiar dance. As soon as she attacked me it was open season. I attacked back."

"Partners feed off each other and keep the low road game going," Alicia added. "The result is that you never learn to do anything differently. The next time a similar situation arises it'll be the same old pattern. Taking the low road is like living in a hamster cage, you spin around on that wheel forever but you never get anywhere."

Tom walked up behind Alicia and wrapped his arms around her waist. He spoke to the group over her shoulder. "Sometimes it's really hard to be kind and respectful but the results are worth it. We'll role-play how this scene might unfold at our house today:" Tom sat back down at the imagined computer:

Alicia: Hi, honey, I had a horrible day.
Tom: *Looks up, smiles and pauses at the keyboard.*
Alicia: I really need to talk.
Tom: Right now?
Alicia: Right now.
Tom: Okay. *Tom turns around and takes Alicia's hand.* Let's go sit on the couch.

Tom and Alicia turned to the group. "Notice that Tom didn't jump up the minute I said that I had a horrible day, but he did smile and pause," said Alicia.

"I'm no saint," he grinned.

Match!

"But what's important is that his behavior didn't throw me off. I needed to talk so I asked for what I wanted."

"I was slow on the uptake," added Tom, "but once I got it, I was all hers. Alicia is way more important to me than a computer game."

Hmmm, thought Sarah. Ask for what you want. I think I can do that.

"Here's another situation involving an everyday moment. Alicia invited me to join her in looking at the sunset. Rather than seizing the opportunity to connect and take the high road, I foolishly took the low road by changing the subject. We'll show you:

Alicia: Tom, look at that beautiful sunset.
Tom: What's for dinner?
Alicia: Fix your own dinner.

"Tom didn't ignore me this time but he ignored what I had to say by changing the subject. It ticked me off and I jumped on the low road with an attack. We're going to try this again:

Alicia: Tom, look at the beautiful sunset.
Tom: What's for dinner?
Alicia: Hungry? Me too. Come look at the sunset and then we'll talk about dinner.

"Alicia took the saint-making opportunity to stay on the high road even though I chose a low road response.

 Match!

She saved the day, or at least the evening. We'll do this one more time so I can show you I'm not a bozo. In this example I'll model what we're encouraging you to do; extend yourself, reach out to your partner every chance you get. Moment-by-moment, comment-by-comment, you're building a strong relationship:

Alicia: Look at the beautiful sunset.
Tom: Wow, it is beautiful. Look at the water. It's magenta.
Alicia: *Sighs as she puts her arms around Tom.*
Tom: Hey honey, I'm getting hungry. Have you any plans for dinner?

The more one judges, the less one loves.
HONORE DE BALZAC

Tom spoke to the couples, "When your mate says something to you–big or small–take a breath, pause and ask yourself: 'How can I join with you and take the high road?' That should be your goal. It helps when you join, it hurts when you attack or ignore. The practice of high road communication is essential even in the smallest of circumstances."

Kate stepped up next to Tom. "Thanks guys for being willing to share some of your real-life experiences. Jim is going to join me in one more example. Many couples have problems around driving. In this fictional role-play, Jim's driving on the freeway in heavy rain, I'm the passenger and we've forgotten about our vows:

Match!

Kate: Slow down. You're driving too fast.
Jim: I know what I'm doing.
Kate: I don't think you do.
Jim: Get off my back.
Kate: How dare you talk to me like that!
Jim: Who's driving?
Kate: You're going to get us both killed. Pull over.

    The room was silent as Jim sat down and Kate spoke, "In this example we were both unconsciously reactive. There is no connecting or acknowledgement of each other's concerns or feelings. We are both lost in a dance of attack, defend, attack again. This can only get worse if we keep it up.

    "Let's explore this further. Please turn in your workbook to the page titled Replay. You can see we started you off with the same freeway scene and the same first two lines. Try to imagine yourself in this situation. Consider the thoughts and feelings that you might experience if you were Kate or Jim. Then fill in the dialogue while attempting to stay kind and respectful."

    This'll be fun, thought Sarah, ever the good student. She wrote:

Kate: Slow down. You're driving too fast.
Jim: I know what I'm doing.
Kate: Jim, I need you to slow down.
Jim: Why?
Kate: Because it's raining really hard and you're driving too fast.

Match!

Jim: I'm only going the speed limit.
Kate: I think that's too fast in this rain.
Jim: Well I don't.

    Sarah could see this wasn't working. As she continued to write, her shoulder knotted up. She hunched over crossing her arms and pressing them against her stomach. How do couples keep from arguing over all the little stuff that happens? She remembered being seven years old, crammed into the backseat of the family car between her brother and sister, her parents battling in the front. She drew a deep breath and dropped her pen on her workbook. There just aren't any pat answers in the real world. People fight!

    Sarah felt a gentle hand on her shoulder. She looked up to see Kate smiling with compassion. "Any comments?" asked Kate, looking around the room.

    A large red-faced man replied. "This was a scene right out of our life. We get in an argument every time we drive on the freeway."

    "Yeah..." the short blond women beside him cut in. "Do I just let him pass the exit? If I say something, he gets mad."

    "I don't know why I get mad, but I do," said the man.

    See, thought Sarah. It's hopeless!

    "Thanks for your honesty," said Kate. "You, like most of us are perhaps carrying around a load of anxiety and anger, much of it unconscious and unexpressed. Anxiety and anger are powerful emotional energies. If they aren't

expressed in appropriate and constructive ways, they can become irrational and nasty. That's why we need to wake up to our inner dialogue.

"You saw it with Alicia and Tom in their first scenario. They became angry at each other because their behavior reflected a history of unmet needs. Tom said that it was a 'familiar dance.' The same thing happened with Jim and me in our role-play. Now," Kate squinted to read the man's nametag, "Bill is reporting a similar experience.

"When you're asleep, you lash out; you blame. You don't have control over what you say and do. You are over-reactive and this is usually disrespectful and inappropriate. When you wake up, you have a choice. You can sink into reactivity or you can take the high road and choose to respond with respect—even on the freeway. The high road expands the boundaries of possibility. There's room for change, new energy." Kate gave Sarah's shoulder a pat and walked to the front. "Waking up and taking the high road isn't the easiest choice, but it's the most skillful and it uses your relationship as a spiritual practice. It also results in deeper understanding of your partner, which nourishes both of you. By taking the high road, you create a peaceful spaciousness that allows the grace of God to re-open your hearts to each other. Jim and I will demonstrate the driving scenario using a high road approach:

Kate: Jim, I'm scared. Would you slow down? This reminds me of when I had that bad accident in the rain.

Match!

Jim: You think I'm driving too fast?
Kate: Too fast for my peace of mind. I'd feel safer at about 45. I can hardly see the road.
Jim: *Slows down.* Is this better?
Kate: Much better. Thanks.
Jim: You're welcome.

Do Overs

Lunch! Sarah sped to the burrito bar. She heaped her tortilla high with beans, shredded cheese and a token sprinkle of lettuce and tomatoes. Mike was visiting with Jim so Sarah decided to join Tom and Alicia at the corner table.

"Hi," said Tom. "Have a seat."

"Thank you. Are you we going to hear from you again?"

"Yep," said Tom. "We like helping with these weekends. So what brought you here, Sarah?"

"My boyfriend knows Kate." Sarah rolled her burrito and took a big bite. After a few minutes of happy eating, she was ready to talk again.

"All this stuff about managing conflict and working with differences makes me nervous. Part of me loves it and part of me thinks it's impossible. Kate and Jim are so civilized when they disagree. In my family it was kill or be killed."

"My family, too," said Tom. "But Alicia was patient and I was determined to make our marriage work."

 Match!

Alicia smiled.

"So, you guys are masters at conflict resolution," said Sarah.

Alicia laughed. "Not always on the first try."

"What do you do?"

"We start over."

"You're already mad and you can still start over? How does that work?" Sarah only knew about arguments that escalated until the combatants retired to lick their wounds, alone.

"We take a mulligan," said Alicia. "Do you know what that is?"

"A stew?"

"Well, that too, but it's a golf term. Tom, tell Sarah about it while I eat. Looks like you two are at least through with your first round."

Tom began. "Sometimes recreational golfers offer each other a mulligan. It's the chance to do a bad shot over without penalty. Alicia and I've discovered that this also works in relationships. Once in awhile I revert to bad habits and make a nasty remark to Alicia. Then I ask for a mulligan."

"Or I suggest he take one," offered Alicia. "I give him a chance to do it over."

"As soon as she asks if I'd like a mulligan, I usually realize the stupidity of my remark. But it goes both ways. Sometimes Alicia needs a mulligan, too."

Forgiveness is the fragrance that the violet sheds on the heel that crushed it.
MARK TWAIN

Match!

Alicia nodded. "Neither of us is perfect."

"That's the truth," said Tom. "For example, we had season tickets to the theater. It was 7:30, the play started at 8:00, and Alicia was still getting ready. I'd been ready for 30 minutes. I looked at my watch, stomped into the bedroom and demanded, 'What's taking so long? We're gonna be late!' Alicia picked up her purse and said with a smile, 'Would you like a mulligan?' I stopped and realized that I sounded just like my Dad shouting at my Mom. Whether or not Alicia was ready, I didn't need to yell about it. Yelling doesn't get me the results I want. So I told her I was sorry. The mulligan kept things from getting out of hand."

"What could you have said instead?" asked Sarah. "I mean if you were really late?"

"Hmm...I might have tried something like this: 'Uh, Alicia, it's getting late and I thought we were going to leave earlier. I'm worried about missing the opening act. How much more time do you need?'" Tom grinned at Sarah. "See, I'm practicing the third vow: I speak honestly with kindness and respect."

Alicia patted Tom on the head and laughed. "We're laughing at ourselves but, bottom line, this stuff works."

Sarah was impressed. "Did you learn to do the mulligan thing from Jim and Kate?"

"Yes," Tom continued. "We needed a code word to ask for a do-over, a chance to take something back. 'Mulligan' works for us."

"Hey, little girl, wanna cookie?" Sarah smiled at the

Match!

familiar voice behind her. Mike slid a fat chocolate chip cookie onto her plate. "I immediately thought of you," he said, sitting down.

"You know you're feeding my addiction," mumbled Sarah, her mouth already full.

"Want me to stop?" asked Mike.

"I'll let you know." Sarah tossed the half-eaten cookie into the pile of leavings on her plate. "By the way, you missed the mulligan."

"They had burritos *and* a stew?"

Inner Dialogue

"Welcome back," Jim boomed inviting people to their seats. "Let me give you a preview of what you'll be doing through the remainder of the weekend. This afternoon we'll focus on hearing and responding to your inner dialogue as part of the awakening process. Then you'll build on this skill by using it in a problem-solving situation with your partner. We're having dinner at 7:00 and then joining Katie at 8:30 for a fireside chat. The topic is passion and spirituality. Following Katie's chat we'll have a question and answer period. The panel will include Tom and Alicia, Katie and me and Joe and Barb—another couple who facilitate these retreats.

"To be an effective communicator, you need to hear and evaluate your own inner dialogue," Jim said. "Your inner dialogue consists of the thoughts and feelings inside your head. When you can identify and understand your

Match!

dominant thoughts and feelings, you're better able to respectfully disclose them to your partner. You also tend to make more skillful behavior choices, often eliminating the actions that cause conflict and turbulence."

Jim continued. "In my first marriage it was a major problem. Since I wasn't paying attention to what I was feeling and thinking, the same arguments repeated with monotonous regularity. My communication was often unkind and disrespectful, not a safe way to process problems. By comparison Katie and I regularly share our thoughts and feelings, which helps us understand our own inner dialogue. We can think out loud, using each other as a sounding board. This is how we head-off misunderstanding and minimize conflict. We're going to teach you how to do this.

"First, please turn to the page titled Feeling Words. *(See Figure 6.)* This is a list of words that describe feelings and the physical cues that often signal a strong emotional reaction. You may want to reference it as you do the exercise on the following page."

I'm glad we're getting a list, thought Sarah. When it comes to expressing feelings, I'm a clam.

Kate stepped forward. "This self-awareness exercise is the first step on what we call 'walking the heart path' of communication. You'll explore the facts in any given situation and your personal biases reflected in your inner dialogue. Separating the facts from opinions will allow you to talk to your partner with more clarity, honesty and respect. This expands your understanding of each other.

 Match!

You'll also be able to see beyond your personal history and habitual reactions, opening to choose a high road collaborative solution. Conflict can evolve into something easier to manage or it can go away entirely.

"We'll begin by recalling a situation between you and your partner when you had a strong negative reaction. For example, your partner is late for a special occasion." Kate smiled and looked around the room. "I can see the wheels turning."

Sarah remembered when Mike was late picking her up for a concert.

"Then I'll ask you some specific questions about the incident. You'll write your answers and we'll go back over them, unthreading the tapestry of reactions you might have experienced. We'll revisit the experience by way of the heart path. Everyone ready?" The group smiled, pens in hand.

"Good. Please write about your situation in the following way. First, describe the facts, what you saw, heard, said or did as objectively as possible in one or two sentences."

Sarah wrote: I had expensive tickets to a concert at Key Arena. Mike was supposed to pick me up at 7:00. At 7:45 he still hadn't arrived, hadn't called.

"Next," said Kate, "write a sentence or two

You cannot solve a problem at the level of thinking that created the problem.
ALBERT EINSTEIN

Feeling Words

❖

LOVING	SAD	MAD	GLAD
adored	dejected	angry	animated
appreciated	depressed	annoyed	awed
aroused	despondent	bitter	blissful
beautiful	disappointed	belligerent	cheerful
cherished	discouraged	cranky	comfortable
delighted	disheartened	enraged	content
effervescent	dismal	furious	ecstatic
enchanting	dismayed	incensed	elated
grateful	dreadful	indignant	enthusiastic
horny	flat	infuriated	exhilarated
kind	gloomy	irate	frisky
loveable	hurt	irritated	gleeful
respected	moody	offended	happy
inspired	mournful	provoked	joyous
joyful	pathetic	resentful	light
jubilant	sorrowful	sarcastic	merry
peaceful	somber		sparkling
playful	unhappy		

Figure 6

Feeling Words

❖

AFRAID	CURIOUS	BRAVE	CONFUSED
alarmed	concerned	audacious	bewildered
anxious	engrossed	bold	displaced
apprehensive	excited	certain	hesitant
chicken	fascinated	confident	inattentive
cowardly	inquisitive	courageous	indecisive
fearful	interested	decisive	perplexed
frightened	intrigued	encouraged	uncertain
hesitant	nosy	heroic	upset
insecure	shocked	reassured	
nervous	stunned	resolute	
panicked	surprised	secure	
petrified	suspicious	self-reliant	
scared			

Physical Cues

❖

light-headed	upset/knotted stomach	drowsy
sweaty	heart skips a beat	dizzy
cold hands	difficulty breathing	chilled
headache	tightness: neck, back	nausea
diarrhea	flooded with warmth	restless
speechless	throat constricted	tears
blood rushing	itchy/sweaty palms	hot

Figure 6

Match!

describing what you thought about the situation."

This was easy. Sarah wrote: I thought that if the concert started on time, I'd missed the first couple of numbers. Why hadn't he called? I wanted to yell at him and tell him off. Then I started wondering if he'd been in a wreck.

"Now, identify and write down the feelings and possibly the physical cues you experienced at the time the situation occurred. For example, frustrated is a feeling and a headache is a physical cue."

Sarah rubbed her forehead and turned back to the feeling words list. This wasn't so easy. She chose 'angry' and 'worried' from the feeling words and 'restless' from the physical cues. Her anxiety increased as she remembered the details of that night. The phone finally rang and Mike explained he was stuck in the emergency room with one of his soccer players. Sarah's anger evaporated before she had the chance to do any damage. Embarrassed, she wrote a little note to Mike at the bottom of the workbook page: I bet you're surprised to read this. If I'd have actually yelled at you, I wonder how you'd have reacted?

Sarah pushed her book towards Mike and then pulled it back, her brows furrowed.

"That bad?" asked Mike.

"We'll see," she sighed, pushing it toward him again.

Mike opened the book and began reading. Suddenly his eyes widened, "No WAY!"

Sarah's heart jumped into her throat.

"Fooled you," he grinned.

 Match!

"Oh stop." She gave him a thin smile. As he continued to read, she tapped her fingers lightly on the table. Finally he spoke, serious for once. "I didn't know you were so angry."

"Well, when I learned what was happening, I wasn't angry anymore. But what if I'd gone ballistic? What would you do?"

"I have to admit I don't do well with yelling or name calling," said Mike. "My parents didn't yell."

"My parents did. And I might."

"Let me put it this way—if yelling was your usual way of communicating, our relationship would be in trouble. But Sarah, you don't scream and yell."

"I haven't so far, but I can feel the tendency inside me. I could very well sink into my family pattern. If you admit you can't handle it, why should we bother getting married?"

"Now we know why we're here," Mike said. He put his hand over hers and they both remained quiet until Kate called everyone back.

"This exercise often brings up fear, confusion, or other feeling reactions to entrenched relationship problems. Honest communication includes learning how to share these thoughts and feelings with your partner. Don't try to come to a solution yet. If you're feeling anxious or overwhelmed, don't worry. We're only half way down the path." Kate smiled.

Walking the Heart Path

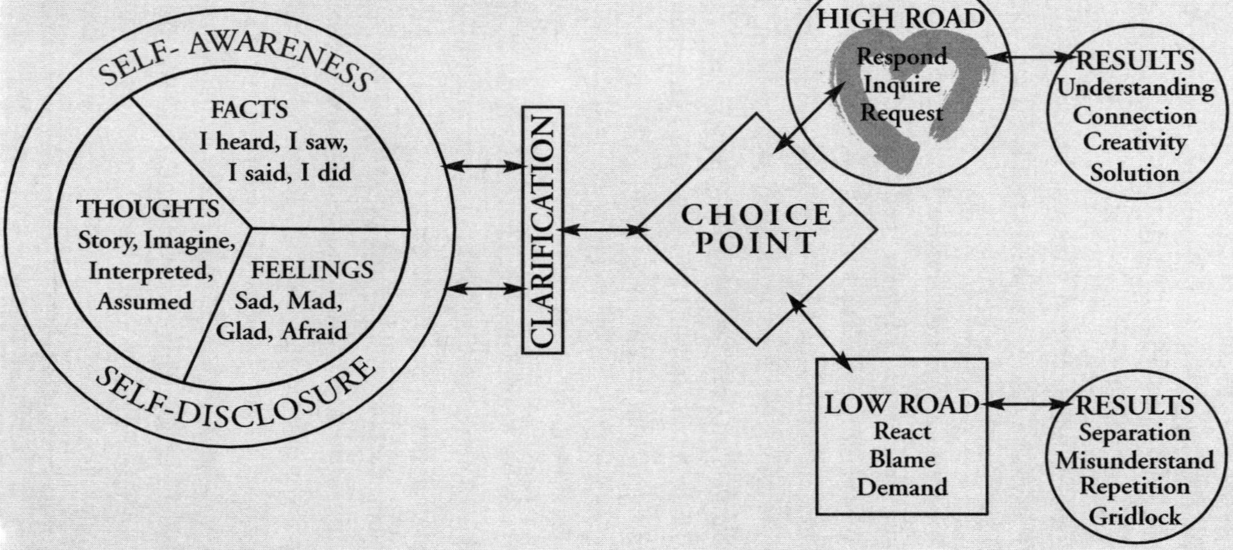

Figure 7

Match!

Walking the Heart Path

"The exercise you just did was for the purpose of increasing self-awareness and understanding, the first step on the heart path," said Kate. She placed a white cardboard chart on the easel. *(See Figure 7.)*

"This is a diagram of walking the heart path. You have it in your workbook." Kate pointed to the large, segmented circle on the chart. "By clarifying the facts and your thoughts and feelings around them, you gained a strong sense of what actually happened and your reaction to it. You're now in a position to make a choice." She pointed to the diamond shape labeled 'choice point.'

"I'd like a volunteer to go through their exercise with me using this chart. But this time, we'll take the heart path all the way to the end." Kate pointed to the circles labeled results. "Who's game?"

The room buzzed. A hand waved from the back of the room. "I will!"

"Ah, a brave soul." Kate motioned to a round, confident-looking young woman. "Come up and bring your workbook with you."

"Go get'em, Sweetie," called a man from the back.

"Everyone, this is Gloria and that voice is her husband, Dan. Thanks for volunteering, Gloria. Please read your description of what was happening in your situation."

Gloria read, "My husband's ex-wife is a total flake. Every time it's her turn to take care of the kids, she is late picking them up. We always have to change our plans to

accommodate her." Gloria stopped reading and looked at Kate.

"Thanks." Kate put her hand on Gloria's shoulder and smiled. "Are you open to some feedback?"

Gloria cleared her throat. "Uh, yeah."

"You're sure? You can always change your mind, you know." Kate chuckled.

"Nope," said Gloria. "That's why I'm here."

"Your statement is too general. Can you describe a particular incident when you changed your plans to accommodate Dan's ex-wife?"

Gloria closed her eyes and began to speak. "Two weeks ago we were waiting for Suzanne." Gloria opened her eyes, looked at Kate and said, "That's his ex-wife's name."

"Got it," said Kate.

Gloria closed her eyes again. "I was sitting on the couch with the kids reading them a story. The phone rang. It was Suzanne. She said that she had to work late and wouldn't be able to pick the kids up on time. I ended up missing my gym date with Dan. I was so..."

"Stop right there, Gloria. I want to compare this description with what you wrote in your workbook." Kate reached for the book. "May I?" she asked.

Gloria handed it to her. Kate glanced down at the open page.

"You wrote that Suzanne was a flake."

Gloria glanced up at Dan as Kate continued. "That's what you think about Suzanne. That's your opinion. However, the first step in this self-awareness exercise asks

you to describe the situation objectively, without judgment or opinion."

Gloria looked confused.

Kate was reassuring. "You wrote that Suzanne is late every time. Is she always late?"

"No," said Gloria.

"Do you always have to change your plans?"

"Not always."

"But maybe half the time she's late?" asked Kate.

Gloria looked up and sighed, "More."

"But not every time."

"No. Not every time."

Kate spoke to the group. "What I'm doing is helping Gloria clarify the facts about what happened. We're removing opinions, interpretations and conclusions; they comprise the story that Gloria's telling herself. For example, the statement 'Suzanne was late' is a fact. The statement 'Suzanne is always late' is Gloria's story, her conclusion. I'm not saying Gloria is wrong or that drawing conclusions is wrong. All I'm saying is that the first step in the awakening exercise doesn't include your interpretations or stories. They come later. Make sense, Gloria?"

Gloria smiled. "Yes—as long as I get to keep my story."

Kate lifted one eyebrow. "We'll see..." She turned back to the group. "Being objective means describing what you saw, heard, said and did. It's helpful to avoid words such as every, always, never and constantly. These all-inclusive words are red flags telling you that you've slipped from objective description into subjective opinion. You've gone from facts to story.

Match!

"We're giving you five minutes to edit your first statement if you found that it was more story than fact." Kate sat down next to Jim.

Sarah checked her notes and sat back satisfied. She was pretty good at recounting facts.

Kate returned to the front of the room. "Now we'll talk about the next part of self-awareness." She pointed to thoughts on the chart. "Gloria, will you read what you thought about this situation with Suzanne?"

"Suzanne is selfish," Gloria read. "She puts work before her children. I think that this is hard on them." Gloria stopped and looked at Kate.

"Excellent Gloria," said Kate. "Next we're going to talk about feelings." She pointed to the corresponding point on the chart. "We'll have Gloria read what she wrote."

Gloria read, "I felt mad, disappointed and sad for the kids."

"That's a good description of feelings," said Kate.

"Okay but I still don't know where we're going with this," said Gloria.

"Remember this is an exercise about waking up to your inner dialogue. Once you're aware of what you're thinking and feeling, you can make a informed decision about what to do next."

Kate again turned to the group. "Gloria has separated her story from the facts. She's now standing at the choice point." Kate pointed to the diamond shape on the diagram. "What she chooses to do next will make all the difference, but first let's explore what happened while

Match!

Gloria was still caught in her story." Kate turned to Gloria. "Do you remember what you did after Suzanne's phone call?"

Gloria shook her head. "Sure. After talking to Suzanne I played with the kids until she came to get them. Dan called from the gym and said he'd meet me at home."

"And how were you feeling inside?" asked Kate.

"Fine as long as I was reading to the kids but once they started playing I thought about the workout I was missing and wondered if steam was coming out my ears. I wanted to complain but the children were in the room."

"Good for you, Gloria," said Kate. "You were emotionally mature in front of the children."

"It didn't feel good," said Gloria

"It may not have felt good but it was a wise decision. Congratulations for pushing the pause button in the heat of the moment. You didn't put the children in the middle; they love both parents. Keep in mind that sometimes it's appropriate to work through conflict in front of your children. What really matters is how and when. In this situation it wasn't a proper time. But modeling healthy and respectful ways of resolving conflict gives children valuable tools for their own lives."

"I didn't do so well with Dan," Gloria admitted.

"Please tell us about that."

"By the time he came home the kids were gone. As soon as he walked in the door I told him what a flake Suzanne was and how angry I was. I think I said that she'd made me miss my workout and that he needed to call her

Match!

right now. I might have been yelling." She looked at Dan. "Was I yelling?"

Dan said, "Yes, you were."

"Okay," said Kate. "This is good stuff to work with."

"Thanks." Gloria rolled her eyes and grinned. "Can I go now?"

"Sure, but we're going to keep talking about it."

Gloria took her seat to a round of applause.

"When Dan came home, Gloria was standing at the choice point. She could take the high road," Kate pointed to the diagram, "or the low road. Can anyone tell me which direction she chose?"

"The low road!" roared Dan. Gloria covered her face with her hands.

"Gloria expressed her feelings in a reactive manner," explained Kate, "blaming Suzanne and making demands on Dan." Kate looked at Dan. "Dan, how did you respond?"

"I refused to call Suzanne," said Dan. "Gloria and I got into a big argument."

"Sounds like you both chose the low road. When you do, you're guaranteed a bad result."

Sarah knew all about the low road. She wanted to hear about the high road.

"If we were working with Dan and Gloria in an individual session, we'd first coach Gloria to state the facts. Then she would honestly and respectfully disclose her thoughts and feelings to Dan. Dan's job would be to graciously listen and support her. Then they could collaborate on a high road choice."

Match!

Inside-Out Communication

"People tend to focus on thinking; they neglect or suppress feelings—especially during relationship turbulence," Kate explained. "However, it's through the sharing of feelings that we build and deepen intimacy. This is how a successful marriage is cultivated. For example, if Jim had to respond to a work emergency just as we were leaving for a dinner date, I might say, 'I know this is your job but I'm sad and disappointed, even a little angry that we can't go to dinner together.' Notice that I don't rant and rave about his stupid job, but I do let him know that I like spending time with him and that I'm unhappy when it doesn't work out.

"Jim and I are now going to demonstrate using the heart path to manage a sudden upset. Gloria, do you mind if we continue to work with your situation?"

Gloria gave the 'thumbs up' sign from her seat.

"We're going to pretend we're Dan and Gloria," said Kate.

"Saturday night at the Improv," said Jim, joining Kate at the front of the room.

"Let's pretend that Dan has just walked through the door," said Kate.

Kate: I need to talk to you about Suzanne.
Jim: Sure, just let me put my stuff down and order Chinese take-out.
Kate: *Brightening.* Sounds good.

Match!

Kate turned to the room. "Notice how Jim is already being supportive."

Jim: *Pretends to make a phone call.* The food will be here in a half hour.
Kate: That should be enough time. Let me tell you what's going on. *Pointing to the Facts on the chart.* Suzanne agreed to pick up the kids at 6:00.
Jim: What time did she finally get here?
Kate: 7:30. *Points to facts.* I was so mad I wanted to spit. *Points to feelings.*
Jim: That mad, eh? *Jim points to clarification, then reaches over and rubs Kate's back.*
Kate: *Kate points to feelings.* And I was disappointed. *Points to thoughts.* I was looking forward to working out with you and then going to dinner.
Jim: *Points to feelings.* I was disappointed, too.

Kate turned to the room. "I've been heard. My feelings are validated. Now I can make a choice to move forward."

Kate: *Points to choice point.* Okay, instead of trashing Suzanne any more, I want to take the high road and make a request. *Points to the heart shape.* Would you talk to her about keeping her agreements?
Jim: *Points to results.* I'll talk to her when I pick-up the kids on Sunday. I hear the doorbell. You ready to eat?
Kate: I'm famished.

Match!

Kate spoke to the group. "The situation was the same, but the outcome changed. We took the high road by following the heart path. I shared the facts unclouded by my story. I was honest about my thoughts and feelings. Jim graciously listened to me. He asked clarifying questions and supported and encouraged me. He rubbed my back. All of this added up. His words and behavior helped me feel better because he was nurturing. This enabled me to disclose my anger without acting it out. If Jim had tried to talk me out of my feelings…"

Jim cut in. "You shouldn't get so angry. You know how she is."

"…I would have become angrier. I might feel put-down rather than supported.

"If you notice yourself taking the low road, try to internally walk the heart path before talking. It's often your story, not the facts, that leads to a low road emotional reaction. Once you look at the facts, your story may change for the better. When your story changes, your reaction changes. The upset may disappear and with it the need to talk. You've successfully coached yourself to a new level of awareness.

"In any case, your emotional reactivity won't dictate your response. You may still be upset and rightfully so, but your increased understanding will often awaken you to a high road solution.

"Now a word about urgency. When you're emotionally charged everything seems urgent. The desire to expel your thoughts and feelings is almost overwhelming.

Match!

Unfortunately, you're in no state to be rational, kind or respectful. A good rule of thumb in relationships is, if it seems urgent—pause.

"Walking the heart path isn't always easy. The low road of habit is well paved and visible. By contrast, the heart path is a trail that you can barely see. It takes clear intention and refocusing to remember your decision to stay on it. But the good news is that the heart path wants to be trod. It widens every time you choose it. After a few structured hikes, walking the heart path becomes second nature."

"And, if you blow it with your partner, you can always apologize and ask for a do-over," said Jim.

Ah, this is where the mulligan comes in. Sarah remembered her conversation with Tom and Alicia.

"So the heart path can be used three ways," Kate continued.

- Alone, increasing self-awareness and understanding of a current or past situation.
- With your partner on the spur of the moment, managing everyday upsets and sudden challenges.
- With your partner in a planned meeting, processing an ongoing or recurring problem.

We must develop and maintain the capacity to forgive. He who is devoid of the power to forgive is devoid of the power to love.
MARTIN LUTHER KING, JR.

 Match!

"You've seen us walk the heart path together and now it's your turn. We're going to give you ten minutes to confer and choose a situation to process. Please don't pick your biggest challenge. Remember, you're still new at this. Choose a topic that you both want to explore."

Sarah yawned. "I just want to explore sleep."

"Me too," said Mike, "but I think we need to do the exercise. Got an idea?"

"How about our summer plans?"

"You mean your love of solitude versus my Grand Canyon extravaganza?"

The chime rang. "First, you're going to write independently about the situation you chose. The writing portion of this exercise will last about twenty minutes. You'll write the facts of the situation. Then you'll describe your thoughts and feelings. You'll conclude with a choice. This could be a high road solution or simply the recognition that you need to process this further.

"Use one of your heart path practice sheets to help you separate facts from your story. We'll call time when the writing period is over."

Sarah's left shoulder tensed as she began to write. Her body was already getting defensive. Good thing the worksheet guided her through the heart path steps. Sarah wrote:

Facts: When I vacation, I like to relax quietly alone or with Mike, maybe with a friend. Mike prefers rugged trips with lots of socializing. He wants to go camping in the Grand Canyon with thirty people.

Match!

Thoughts: I like people, just not in herds. I hope Mike doesn't think I'm being obstinate. It seems to me that if I go with him to the Grand Canyon, I'll have to take a vacation to recover from my vacation.

Feelings: I feel overwhelmed when I'm with too many people for too long. Right now I feel tired because I've been around people all weekend. I'm angry with myself because I can't just rise to the occasion and be more willing to do the crowd thing. I'm scared that we won't last because of this difference. I feel sad.

Choice Point: I'll look at this from the high road since I've already spent enough time on the low road.

High Road: I'm going to respond and inquire. I don't know how but I'll try to listen graciously to what he has to say and I know he'll listen to me. My heart and my mind are open.

Results: We'll feel closer because we've shared and, like Joe and Barb, maybe we'll have a shift in consciousness.

Time was called.

"Now you get to walk the heart path together," Jim said. "Go back to your room or spread out in the lodge and take turns reading what you wrote to your partner. When you're finished reading, turn to your vows and then to your gracious listening page. Read over both of these before you begin your discussion. Keep heading toward the high road. If it helps, point to the step on the heart path that you're addressing. For example, if you need to clarify a fact, you could point to facts on the diagram. If you have a feeling to share, you could point to feelings. Regardless,

Match!

what counts here is not the pointing; it's the communicating. And as you talk to each to each other don't forget the following guidelines:

- Try to stay physically close, give a gentle touch, a hand squeeze.
- If things get too hot, call a time-out until you can think more clearly.
- See your situation as a spiritual path. It is here to help you grow. This keeps your discussion aimed toward solution, healing and understanding.
- Weigh your behavior against the vows. Keep them in the forefront.
- If you've reached the end of your rope, don't give up. Find a someone to help you through the rough spots. Counseling is useful when people are stuck.

"Remember, you don't have to resolve the problem today—just try to increase your understanding of each other. We'll be available if you'd like to consult with us."

Heart Path Solutions

Sarah and Mike decided to stay in the main room in case they needed help. Sarah read what she had written to Mike and then Mike read to Sarah:

Facts: I have the opportunity to go on a two-week rafting trip on the Grand Canyon this summer. I'll get continuing education credits. I'd like Sarah to go along. Sarah doesn't want to go.

Match!

Thoughts: Sarah is just shy. I think that if she'd try it, she'd like it. If I give in and don't go myself, I'll be making compromises for the rest of my life.

Feelings: I feel torn between wanting to go on the trip and wanting to please Sarah. I feel sad that I can't share the rafting experience with her. I feel angry that she won't give it a try.

Choice Point: I choose to look for an answer that will work for both of us.

High Road: We'll have to try and figure this out together because I haven't got a clue.

Results: She'll realize that the trip will be fun.

When Mike finished, Sarah pointed to feelings on the diagram. "I'm annoyed and sad." She moved her finger to clarification. "You think I'm shy. If I'd try the camping trip, I'd like it. "

"That's right," said Mike. "And now you feel sad and annoyed?"

"Yes, I do."

"Tell me why."

Sarah pointed to thoughts. "Because you don't understand me at all." Her voice rose. "I'm not shy."

Again she pointed to feelings. "It's not shyness, it's exhaustion. I feel exhausted when I'm around too many people for too long. Like now, I'm really tired. I'd like to go upstairs and sleep for hours."

Mike pointed to feelings. "I feel frustrated."

He pointed to thoughts. "I guess I don't understand what's it's like to be you."

Match!

He pointed to choice point. "I want to take the high road but I don't know how to fix this. Let's ask Kate about it."

"Okay," Sarah sighed, rubbing her shoulder.

Mike stood up and walked over to Kate. "We're stuck," he said.

"Let's take a look," said Kate.

Mike and Kate walked back over to Sarah. Kate pulled up a chair, sat down next to them and asked, "How can I help?"

Sarah and Mike shared what they'd written. "This is a tough one," she said. "You see, extroverts are usually energized by being with lots of people. Introverts are frequently depleted by groups and recharge themselves by being quiet. These are basic characteristics that need to be honored."

Sarah sagged in her chair.

"Don't despair." Kate patted Sarah's knee. "There are two keys to working with differences: understanding and acceptance." Kate looked at each of them in turn. "From the sharing you've already done, you may have gained more understanding. Do you think you have?"

"I have," Mike said. "I've always thought shy people needed someone to bring them out of their shell."

"Mike," Sarah interrupted. "I'm not shy."

"Okay, Sarah. That's my story. I've been thinking of introverts as shy for a long time. You're not shy; you're an introvert."

"And proud of it." Sarah smiled, resting her hand on his.

Match!

Mike's face softened. "I'm trying to turn you into someone you're not. I'm hurting, not helping." Mike turned to Kate. "So where do we go from here?"

"Well," Kate glanced at Mike's workbook, "you wrote that you were concerned about making compromises for the rest of your life."

"I am."

"If you go on the trip and Sarah doesn't go, would you consider that a compromise?"

"Yes."

"What are you compromising?" asked Kate.

Mike looked down at the floor and was quiet before speaking. "I'm losing the joy of sharing the experience with her."

"So because you can't make Sarah come with you, your experience is compromised?"

"Somewhat."

"What if she went with you, in order to make you happy and then she was miserable for two weeks?"

"That would be even worse. I want her to go and I want her to like it."

"So you want to control her behavior and her feelings as well."

Mike smiled. "That sounds pretty lame."

"Mike," said Kate, "a major cause of chronic unhappiness in relationships is trying to change your partner's basic characteristics and then expecting her to thank you for it."

Sarah leaned forward. "So what's the answer Kate? Is

Match!

there something I need to do?"

"You tell me," said Kate. "But here's a clue, it involves consideration. Consideration feels good. It doesn't include compromise. Compromise feels bad."

"We've talked about Mike going without me and then the two of us going to the coast for a week, alone," said Sarah.

"That's an idea," said Kate.

"But I'm not sure I want him to be gone for two weeks without me."

"So?" asked Kate.

Sarah closed her eyes. "I don't want Mike pushing me into something I don't want to do." She opened her eyes and with a faint smile, continued. "In all fairness, I shouldn't try to keep him from doing something he wants to do."

"Makes sense," Kate agreed.

"Wait a minute. I just realized something," said Mike, "I want epoch shared experiences."

"Epoch? What does that mean?" asked Sarah.

"Big. We've had big experiences without each other. I'd like to have some together. I've always thought of a raft trip down the Colorado River as an epoch event."

"I'd like to take a raft down the Colorado," said Sarah. "It's the thirty people for two weeks that freaks me out."

"Considering that Sarah would like to share this epoch experience, just not with thirty people, how might you restructure your plans?" Kate asked.

"Hmm...okay," said Mike, "I'll think out loud here.

Match!

There are a slew of outfitters offering river trips. Sarah and I could go on the Internet and look over the options. Maybe I could still get credits for it."

"How does that sound, Sarah?" asked Kate.

"Interesting," said Sarah. "A boutique rafting experience. I feel excited."

Mike sat back in his chair. "This might work."

"It will," said Kate, as she rose to leave.

Commitment

At break time Sarah and Mike walked hand in hand up the stairs and into their room. "You okay?" he asked, closing the door behind him.

"Yeah, I'm tired. That was a lot to take in." Sarah flopped down on the bed. Mike slipped off his shoes and lay down next to her.

"How about if we relax for a while?" she said. "I need some quiet."

"Ah yes, the introvert needs to recharge. Actually, I'd like that too."

They both studied the ceiling. Sarah spoke after several minutes. "It's funny. We have some fundamental differences in our personalities but it doesn't seem wrong."

No response.

"I mean, even though we're far apart in our social needs, I feel closer to you than ever."

Still no response.

"Mike?" Sarah rolled to her side and propped her head

up with her hand.

Mike's mouth curled in a half-smile and his eyelids fluttered slightly. His breathing was calm and deep. Hmmm, Sarah wondered, is he dreaming about camping in the Grand Canyon or me?" She leaned in close, her lips grazing his ear.

"Poor extrovert," she whispered. "You need this quiet time even more than I do." She draped her free arm over his chest and felt her body relax as she snuggled against him.

A sharp laugh outside the door startled Sarah awake. She glanced at her watch. An hour until dinner. She felt Mike next to her and pressed into him, tracing the contours of his exposed ear with her finger. "Hey there, sleepy head," she whispered, "are you ready to rise and shine?"

Mike gently pulled her hand to his lips. "I'll let you know after I've consulted with ten of my closest friends," he said, nibbling her fingertips. Then he rolled over and kissed her softly, lingering at the nape of her neck.

"Ah yes," she murmured as he trailed down her shoulder. "The extrovert needs to, uhmmmm, socialize." Suddenly her stomach rumbled.

"I'm glad to hear I have such a stimulating effect," Mike said, lifting his head.

"Sorry," she rubbed her belly. "I really want to talk."

"Now she wants to talk," he groused. Her stomach growled again, louder this time. "Sounds like you need to eat."

Sarah ran her hands over her t-shirt, smoothing the

Match!

wrinkles. "Sometimes other issues take precedence," she smiled. "But I would like to talk on another topic." She sat up.

"Which topic?" Mike was always suspicious when Sarah wanted to do something besides eat.

"Well, I was thinking of how you wanted more days of the week with me. And remember my fear of marriage?" She kissed him lightly on the cheek and hopped up from the bed.

"Waaaaait just a minute here." His eyes widened. "Are you bringing up the forbidden subject..." he grabbed his neck and gagged, "marriage?"

Sarah whacked him with her down pillow. "What if I am?" she said. "Maybe we should walk the heart path and see what happens?"

Mike sat up. "Don't toy with me."

Sarah settled down next to him and took his hands into hers. "I'm not teasing. Maybe I don't have to be afraid of personality differences and conflict. Maybe," she gulped, "despite what I've seen, long-term relationships can actually work."

"Who are you and what did you do with my girlfriend?"

"Look Mike, I don't know what to think right now. I'm confused and excited all at the same time. That's why I want to talk about this with you." Sarah looked out the window.

"Okay, I get it." Mike said. "Let me grab the Heart Path diagram."

Anyone can be passionate, but it takes real lovers to be silly.
ROSE DOROTHY FRANKEN

Match!

Sarah shifted on the bed, pressured by his enthusiasm. "Remember, we don't have to resolve anything right now. Let's give ourselves time."

Mike returned with the notebook and opened it to the chart. "Honey, I'm trying not to rush you. But let's face it, I do feel a certain urgency." He pointed to thoughts. "I think that our relationship needs to move forward. I'm ready to get off the fence and if after all this time, you're still stuck, well…" he pointed to choice point.

Sarah pulled his fingers from the page and held them tight. "Let's use the process first," she cautioned. "Then we'll make some choices."

"Okay," Mike calmed down. "I'm ready if you are."

Sarah put her finger on facts. "We love each other and want to spend more time together. For you that means getting married; for me it means you coming over more often. Do you agree those are the facts?"

"Yes," Mike said. "But we've been together over two years now and—I don't mean to be melodramatic—but we aren't getting any younger."

Sarah winced.

"Honey," Mike reached for Sarah's hand. "I want a future. I want commitment. I had hoped that you wanted the same." He pointed to feelings. "I feel very tense right now."

Sarah pointed to the same spot on the diagram, keeping a hold of Mike's hand. Physical closeness seemed important. "I feel the same way. We've talked about it in the past, but never with this kind of clarity. It feels different."

 Match!

"So what's your concern at this point?" Mike asked.

"Mike," Sarah explained, "you know I love you."

Mike smiled. "Yes, I do."

"And you know how I feel about marriage. My observations tell me that it's a hornet's nest of problems. I've got a temper buried somewhere in here and I'm afraid I'll alienate you before the honeymoon's over."

They went silent.

Sarah pointed to thoughts. "What's happening in your head?" She moved her finger to feelings. "I'm worried."

"Well," Mike sighed, "I thought you'd changed your mind. We've learned a lot about turbulence as a natural part of a relationship and we've explored ways to navigate through it. I thought that this weekend opened you up some."

"It did, Mike. That's why we're talking. But it didn't remove my fear. I'm not going to change..." she snapped her fingers, "just like that. I need time."

"You always need time, Sarah." Mike's voice was tired. He dropped her hand. "Okay," he said, resigned. "How much more time do you need?"

"Let's see," she looked at her watch. "How about fifteen minutes?"

"Excuse me?"

"I said," she enunciated carefully, "how about fifteen minutes? It'll take me that long to change into my 'accepting proposal' attire."

Mike blinked hard. "You're serious."

"Oh I still have doubts. But I can see how hiding from

 Match!

commitment is no way to live, especially when I'm blessed to have someone like you in my life." She leaned over and kissed him. A smile slowly spread across his face but he didn't move. "Are you in shock?" she asked.

Mike was mute, but continued to grin.

"Okaaay..." she whispered. "I'll just mosey over to the closet and change my clothes. Maybe after you've recovered, you'll be able to pop the question again."

Mike nodded enthusiastically, still silent. Then he jumped up, pulled his duffel bag from under the bed and sorted through its contents. "Voila!" he cried, his hand upraised in triumph. He was holding a small black box. "I'll meet you in the meadow in fifteen minutes."

"What if I'm late?" Sarah laughed, pulling on her sweatshirt.

"I'll give this to the next woman who crosses my path!" Then he dashed out the door.

Sarah's loafers crunched along the gravel path. I'm stepping into my future she thought and it feels great.

Mike waited on a log bench under a towering cedar. As Sarah approached, he rose and walked toward her. "I'll always meet you half way," he smiled, taking her arm. He guided her back to the bench. Sarah sat down and Mike knelt in the wet grass. Taking her hand into his he said, "Sarah, from the moment we met I've been awed by your intelligence, your beauty and your extraordinary heart. I can't imagine life without you. Will you marry me?"

"I will," she said, eyes misty.

Mike fished the box from his vest, removed the ring

Match!

Marrying for love may be a bit risky, but it is so honest that God can't help but smile on it.
JOSH BILLINGS

and slipped it on her finger. He leaned forward and gently kissed her.

"And there's more." Mike reached into his inside pocket extracting a small gold pouch tied with a red ribbon.

"Belgian chocolates!" she gushed.

"Allow me," said Mike, removing the ribbon and extending the offering to Sarah.

Sarah selected a chocolate and took a bite. She considered the diamond on her left hand, the chocolate in her right. "Hard to decide which I like best."

Passion and Spirituality

Sarah and Mike strolled arm-in-arm from the dining room to the fireplace. Mike whispered in her ear, "It would've been nice to spend the rest of the evening alone."

"I want to get our money's worth." Sarah grinned.

"I think we already have." Mike picked up her left hand and rubbed the ring.

"You're right," she said, twining her fingers in his. They pulled two chairs together and settled down for Kate's fireside chat.

"Good evening," said Kate, perched on a stool in front of the fire. "When we fall in love we experience our spiritual nature. God expresses

Match!

through us as love. At a deep level, we recognize that we are part of a loving universe, a transcendent whole. When a loving couple comes together in a full experience of sexual ecstasy, the physical world disappears and melts into a single point of cosmic bliss. It's a spiritual awakening. Maybe you remember feeling touched by magic, becoming almost a new person. The cynic might say that this is just the reproductive urge, nature's way of guaranteeing the continuance of the species. I disagree. All that's necessary for reproduction is the physical, erotic side of sexual release. The incredible joy of being in love is something above and beyond the physical. It's a glimpse into a higher level of existence.

"So where does all the magic go and how can we get it back? Well, the love hasn't gone anywhere, however the erotic newness will likely fade. Couples who don't understand that this is a natural development—that it has nothing to do with the depth of their love—may interpret it as a sign that the love is evaporating. The media supports this view: you're only truly in love if you can't keep your hands off each other.

"Further, there's an addictive quality to the newness. Beginnings are always exciting and it's not easy to navigate the turbulent transition from new to lasting love. However, when a couple walks the heart path through their challenges, the relationship is no longer driven by excitement. Instead it's continually renewed by a wellspring of understanding, strength and connection. And yes, the sex is still really good." Kate smiled at Jim. "What you're

looking to experience is enduring enthusiasm (from the Greek entheos which means having a god within). Much better than the capricious excitement."

Sarah breathed in Kate's words.

"It's said that if sex is a problem, it accounts for 80% of the quality of the relationship. If it's not a problem, it only rates about 20% of our attention. In other words, when the sex is good then there's lots of energy left to enjoy other delightful aspects of being together. If sex is a problem, it can inundate the relationship and block the good feelings.

"So what can you do? Don't expect to have a full blown, ecstatic experience every time you have sex. Sex is not a performance; it's an opportunity for warmth, closeness and physical release. Sometimes it will last a long time; sometimes it won't. Enjoy each other without rating yourself by the quality of your partner's orgasm. And while I'm on the subject," Kate smiled, "here are a few reminders that merit repeating:

- When you make love, bring your full attention to the act.
- Say yes as often as possible; even brief sexual connections count.
- Let your partner know what you like and what you don't.
- Continue to find new ways to enjoy each other sexually; be playful, laugh, explore.

Match!

- If your partner makes requests that fall outside your comfort zone, say so.
- Show your appreciation with your words, eyes and touch. Bask in the glow.

"For couples who are mentally and physically healthy, it ought to be easy. However, some of you have health issues or emotional traumas that need to be addressed. In these instances, seek professional help. And as you do, don't forget to walk the heart path, sharing your challenges with your partner. Partners need to listen with kindness and compassion. Remember, love heals.

"Sex is sacred. Monogamy of body, mind and heart is a commitment to lasting love and a spiritual practice. It is a practice that builds character centered in the values of trust, loyalty and honesty. When you scatter your sexual energy it's like squandering your wealth, ultimately leaving you bankrupt and lonely. Monogamy allows you to return to the source of your strength as a couple; the warmth, security and fulfillment you have with each other. By holding sex as sacrosanct in your relationship the desire to go elsewhere diminishes, eventually disappearing altogether. When you live the principles and practices that we've talked about this weekend, your relationship will become a

A successful marriage requires falling in love many times, always with the same person.
MIGNON McLAUGHLIN

Match!

sanctuary. It will be the foundation for a fulfilled and meaningful life together. Blessings on you all."

Kate closed her eyes and the group enjoyed a few refreshing minutes of silence.

Questions and Answers

Jim spoke to the group. "We're ready to begin the question and answer session. Joe and Barb have joined us, along with Alicia and Tom." The panelists carried chairs to the front of the room. "Tom has sorted the questions you've written over the course of the retreat. He chose a few that are representative." Tom made a show of searching his pockets and then pulled out several white slips.

"Okay panel, here's the first question," said Tom. He selected a single slip of paper and began to read, "What if you're attracted to someone else?"

"When you notice a sexual thought about someone else," said Kate, "let it go. There's a difference between momentary attraction and an ongoing fantasy. If you entertain the idea long enough, you're likely to act on it. Then it's difficult to build trust again."

"If I have a fleeting moment of attraction," said Joe, "I intentionally think of Barb. Then it pales by comparison." Barb reached over and squeezed Joe's hand.

"By going from attraction to attraction you never develop the deep intimacy and trust possible only through a long-term relationship," said Kate. "It's the addiction to newness and being too lazy to dig for the gold in your

present relationship that creates the seduction. If you're attracted to someone else, you're standing at the choice point. Choose to bring your energy back into the relationship. If this is too difficult, seek counseling right away. Nip it in the bud."

"Let's move on," said Tom, reading another question. "I think my spouse is over-sexed. What is a normal sex drive?" Tom looked up and smiled. "Alicia used to think that about me."

"We worked it out," said Alicia, laughing. "But seriously, he dropped his expectations about how I was supposed to respond. What a relief. Now when I'm not up for a big production and Tom wants to have sex, I can say 'let's make it a quickie.' It's nice to connect physically even when I'm not passionate, and Tom's self-image is no longer tied to my hormonal cycles."

"I'm just happy she says yes," Tom smiled.

"Consideration is the key to dealing with all differences," said Kate. "There is no such thing as a normal sex drive. I mean, who'd get to decide? However, if you have a partner who wants sex several times a day for years, it may mean that they need to get a life." Kate laughed and so did everyone else. Then she paused. "On the other hand, it could indicate a lack of mutual connection on many levels. Perhaps you're emotionally disconnected and your partner is begging for attention. It could also be a physical or psychological problem that needs a professional assessment."

When the panelists finished fielding the written

Match!

questions, Tom opened the floor for general comments. Sarah looked at Mike and ever-so-slightly shook her head 'no'. Mike nodded. Good, she thought, he's respecting our privacy.

Jake spoke, "I'm really sarcastic. I always thought it was funny. But Meagan listed my sarcasm as one of her hot topics so we talked about it. I didn't know how tough it was, being the brunt of my jokes all these years. I'm gonna put a lid on it."

Mike leaned over. "Am I sarcastic?"

Sarah wrinkled her nose. "Uhm, maybe a teensy bit—sometimes. What do you think?"

"I was pretty smart-mouthed in college. Male bonding," said Mike. "When I'm teaching, sometimes it comes out in the classroom."

Sarah raised an eyebrow.

"Yeah, not good," said Mike. "I think I'm being funny but I could be hurting a kid's feelings. I better put a lid on it too."

Nancy spoke next. "I realized that I don't ask for what I want. I want Paul to read my mind and then I get sulky when he doesn't. But part of me is annoyed that I need to do the asking in the first place. After all these years, shouldn't he know a few things without being told? I still wonder if he's just ignoring me."

"Let's start at the beginning, Nancy," said Jim. "You don't ask for what you want. Why not?"

"Because Paul should just know," said Nancy.

"Hmm," said Jim. "Does Paul represent himself as having psychic powers?"

 Match!

Nancy laughed. "Hardly."

"Then you need to ask for what you want. Perhaps Paul wants to know so he can respond, 'yes, no or later.' Regardless of whether Paul does or doesn't want to know, it doesn't serve you to sulk. It's a low road reaction."

"But we've been married twenty-seven years!"

"And in all that time you haven't learned to ask for what you want?"

"You've got a point, Jim. I don't know if I like it but I heard it," said Nancy.

"Nancy, I don't want to put this all on you," said Jim. "But the only person you can change is you."

Paul put his arm around Nancy and drew her close. "We're in this together."

Jim looked at the group. "Sometimes what will help and what you want to hear are not the same. Do what helps."

As the panel continued to comment on other questions, Mike leaned into Sarah and whispered, "I'm brain dead. Mind if we check out?"

"Let's go," said Sarah, thankful for back row seats. They slid out, quietly making their way toward the exit. Once out of view, Sarah flew up the stairs to their room, tossed her clothes in a heap and dove between the covers.

"Looks like I said something in the nick of time," said Mike, stepping into the room.

"It was good stuff but I was nodding off," said Sarah, eyelids at half mast. "I was trying to stay for your sake."

"For me? I was staying for you. Maybe we need to communicate sooner rather than later."

Match!

Sarah turned on her side and curled into an S, closing her eyes.

"Goodnight," said Mike, still standing at the door. "I'll turn out the lights."

"Night," she yawned. "Love you."

Nurture

Sarah's eyes opened to bright morning sunlight and Mike singing in the shower. She buried her face in the pillow next to her, lingering in his aftershave. Then she held her hand up to study the diamond twinkling on her finger.

"Enjoying the ring?" Mike called, leaning out of the shower stall.

Sarah rolled over on her stomach and rested her head in her hands, raising her voice above the hiss of the shower. "I've discovered something about myself."

"Besides the fact that you're crazy about me?"

"I mean something new about myself."

"Enlighten me," he said, returning to his shower.

"I've discovered that I really like being engaged." She sat up. "I can get used to mornings like this."

"What, you in bed and me alone in the shower?"

"No problem," she replied, slipping off her pajamas and tiptoeing toward the bathroom. "I can fix that."

Sarah and Mike barely finished their French toast before it was time to head for the conference room. Jim was waving his arms again, encouraging everyone to be seated. "Good morning!" he announced. "We're heading

Match!

into the final stretch. Today we'll focus on nurturing and anchoring commitment."

Mike squeezed Sarah's hand and she smiled broadly. Commitment felt nice.

"You did good work yesterday," Jim continued. "You walked the heart path and practiced new skills. You put your vows into action. You may have resolved a conflict or maybe you just shared and listened. Either way, you know each other a little better. Can you feel the energy in this room?" He paused briefly. "Loving, respectful communication lifts all of us. The reason we meet someone and decide to spend our lives together is so that love can express in physical form. Your relationship is an opportunity for the grace and love of God to show up and bless the world."

Sarah wondered how many times she'd find herself at the choice point. I hope I remember to take the high road. It works so much better.

"Take a look at your vows," said Jim. "We're going to talk about the fourth statement, I nurture our relationship in thought and deed. It's important to think about your partner in positive ways and to express you're gratitude on a daily basis. Once a week isn't enough. Performing intentional acts of kindness needs to become a lifestyle; a lifestyle that says, 'I'm glad you're in my life.'

"Let me share a few examples. Every evening I ask Katie about her day and sometimes I bring her flowers. Katie and I schedule special time each week just to have fun together. We also set aside time to discuss plans or

Match!

problems. We are continually finding ways to connect and show that we care.

"When we were in the romantic phase of our relationship, these caring acts occurred naturally. As the newness wore off, the caring acts decreased. Then we decided to become intentionally caring. It took effort, but we persisted. Now it's easy again because it has become a habit."

Kate spoke up. "Don't take your partnership for granted. If you neglect it you grow apart. Mutual acts of caring enrich the relationship and nourish both of you."

Jim continued. "Now turn to the page titled Intentional Gifts. You're going to compose two lists. First, write down all the gifts, big or little, that you'd like to receive from your partner. Then list the gifts you'd like to give. For example: love notes, candy, a walk on the beach, the possibilities are endless. But be specific— 'more time together' is too general— 'a date one evening each week' is specific and you'll know if your request has been fulfilled. Write until we call time."

"What a great idea," said Sarah. "I'm always wondering what I can give you that you'd like." Sarah and Mike were still busy writing when the chime rang.

"All right," called Jim, quieting the group.

May no gift be too small to give, nor too simple to receive, which is wrapped in thoughtfulness, and tied with love.
L. O. BAIRD

 Match!

"Exchange books. Using your partner's list, circle the requests that you are willing to fulfill and the gifts you are willing to receive. If appropriate include dates. Items that are not circled can be topics for future discussion. Here's an example. I want to take Katie on a trip to Yosemite. Katie wants to go but not until next spring. Now I have a timeframe for planning."

Sarah and Mike exchanged books, circling their choices.

"Now you each have two list of gifts to give your partner—one in each of your books. Find time during the coming week to combine them into one list for easy reference." *(See Figure 8.)*

"Keep your gift list handy," said Kate. "Everyday you have opportunities to show your partner that you care. Intentional gifts, gracious listening, walking the heart path through conflicts, respecting differences and showing appreciation will invest energy into your relationship, build closeness and trust."

I know about this, thought Sarah.

"Destructive behaviors and negative words are potent trust breakers," Kate warned. "It may take many gifts of kindness to make up for a mean-spirited remark or nasty argument."

Sarah leaned into Mike and whispered, "Please tell me we won't get into nasty arguments. I'd rather live alone for the rest of my life than recreate my childhood."

"Sarah, look at me." Mike's voice was gentle. "If that ever happens, I'll call a time-out so fast," he made a T with his hands, "it'll be over before it starts."

Intentional Gifts for <u>Sarah</u>

Chocolates
Foot massage
Trip to the Oregon coast
Breakfast in bed
Walk through the Arboretum
Wash and vacuum her car
A trip to the Skagit Valley Tulip Festival
Ride the ferry from Seattle-Victoria
Join her to visit her parents once a month
A bottle of Lavender massage oil

Figure 8

Match!

"Promise?"

"I promise."

Sarah looked at the clock. The retreat was almost over and she felt like she was just getting started. At the front of the room, Kate and Jim stood next to each other surveying the group.

Kate spoke, "Coming here this weekend was an act of faith. When you step out in faith, something shifts. Something has shifted forever in your heart and in your relationship. It may be a small change that you hardly notice, but even a slight change in trajectory has enormous ramifications. You may not notice it today, but your future is already altered. The challenge is to maintain and improve upon your new direction. You're no longer simply two individuals trying to get along with each other; you're a spiritual force on a noble quest—the quest for enlightenment through the path of relationship." She paused briefly. "Your mission is to awaken to the wonder of who you are as expressions of the Divine by following the heart path.

"We'll close by saying the vows aloud. Your willingness to keep them from this day forward will make all the difference. Please stand, face each other, join hands and repeat after me:

Love is meant to heal. Love is meant to renew. Love is meant to bring us closer to God.
DEEPAK CHOPRA

 Match!

- I commit fully to our relationship.
- I listen with an open heart and open mind.
- I speak honestly, with kindness and respect.
- I nurture our relationship in thought and deed.

"You have set a miracle in motion. Your relationship has been renewed and it's a blessing to yourselves and your world."

Match!

Epilogue

"Who's that mommy?" Claire pointed to a picture in the photo album.

"Kate and Jim at our wedding. You know Kate and Jim." Claire snuggled next to Sarah on the couch.

"They're dressed funny," said Claire, screwing up her face.

"We're all dressed funny," Sarah explained. "It was Daddy and Mommy's wedding and they were helping us get married." Sarah leaned into the soft cushions.

"You needed help?"

"Well, actually we needed a lot of help. But Kate's a minister, she was performing the ceremony and Jim was helping her." Sarah closed the album and placed it on the coffee table next to a white, china bowl filled with carrots and raisins. Claire plucked two carrots from the bowl and held one up to Sarah's mouth. Sarah wiggled her nose like a bunny, snatched the carrot with her teeth, and chomped. The two of them munched and giggled until Claire turned to Sarah, serious.

"Mommy?" asked Claire.

Match!

"Yes?"

"Does Daddy play with Matt more than me?"

"Do you think that Daddy plays with Matt more than he plays with you?"

"Yes," said Claire, sticking out her lower lip.

"What do you want Daddy to do?"

"I want Daddy to play with me."

"So how can you help that happen?"

"I can ask him!" Claire jumped off the couch, skipped across the living room and out the front door. "Daddy," she sang, "can I talk to you?"

"Sure sweetheart." Mike's voice was gentle. "Come sit with me."

Sarah leaned back absently stroking Sophie as sounds of Mike and the children drifted through the open window. I'm part of a healthy, happy family, she thought. And I eat right.

Weird.

Match!

Afterword

Though every relationship may not turn out to be 'happily ever after,' we believe that every person can live a happier, healthier life. Successful living isn't an accident of birth but instead the result of a series of small choices. How you choose to respond to the variety of events and circumstances in your life will determine the quality of your experience.

Each life is a tapestry of interwoven threads; genetics; family dynamics, temperament, education and character, to name a few. Sarah's tapestry contained a genetic predisposition to addictive eating coupled with a dysfunctional family history. This led her to experience fear, self-doubt and anxiety, even in a caring, supportive relationship.

Mike's appearance in Sarah's life is a mystery that we call 'grace.' When you're willing to step into the opportunities that grace supplies, you tap into the universal love that lies at the center of every life. To fully savor the present and the future you must give up behaviors and stories that are

soothing or cathartic in the moment, but detrimental in the long-run. It isn't easy because the path of least resistance is to maintain the status quo; but perseverance pays off.

Sarah was afraid to marry Mike, but after she understood how her behavior could harm her future, she embraced healing strategies to help her take advantage of her blessings. Sarah's retreat experience was the beginning. It awakened her desire to keep learning about being part of a healthy, happy family.

If we had given Sarah a short, follow-up reading list, this is what it would have been:

Bibliography

Barker, Raymond Charles. *The Power of Decision*. Dodd, Mead & Company, Perigee Books, 1991

DesMaisons, Kathleen. *Potatoes not Prozac* . A Fireside Book, Simon & Schuster,1999.

Gottman, John M. and Nan Silver. *The Seven Principles for Making Marriage Work*. Three Rivers Press, Random House, Inc., 1999.

Groves,Dawn. *Meditation for Busy People and Yoga for Busy People.*. New World Library, 1993.

Keirsey, David. *Please Understand Me II.* Prometheus Nemesis Book Company,1999.

Kornfield, Jack. *A Path With a Heart.* Bantam Books, 1993.

Richo, David. *How to Be an Adult.* Paulist Press, 1991.

Ruiz, Don Miguel. *The Four Agreements.* Amber-Allen Publishing, 1997.

Thompson, Helen. Artwork by Paddy Bruce, *Milagros: A Book of Miracles.* HarperSanFrancisco, 1998.

About the Authors

Rev. Colleen and Bob MacGilchrist bring 26 years of experience in couples counseling and retreats. Colleen is a minister, counselor, couples coach and educator. Bob is a licensed marriage and family therapist and a licensed mental health counselor. He is a clinical member of the American Association for Marriage and Family Therapy. They live in Washington State.

For information about workshops or to order books please contact them directly at:

Heart Path Retreats
Email: info@heartpathretreats.org
Website: www.heartpathretreats.org
Phone: 360.756.1160
Fax: 360.671.4949